CANADIAN SHIELD

CANADIAN SHIELD

KELLEY AITKEN

TIGHTROPE BOOKS

Tightrope Books
#207-2 College Street,
Toronto Ontario, Canada M5G 1K3
tightropebooks.com
bookinfo@tightropebooks.com

EDITORS: Sue MacLeod and Helen Humphreys
COPYEDITOR: Deanna Janovski
COVER DESIGN: Anna Payne-Krzyzanowski
LAYOUT DESIGN: David Jang

Canada Council for the Arts | Conseil des arts du Canada

ONTARIO ARTS COUNCIL
CONSEIL DES ARTS DE L'ONTARIO
an Ontario government agency
un organisme du gouvernement de l'Ontario

Produced with the assistance of the Canada Council for the Arts and the Ontario Arts Council.

Library and Archives Canada Cataloguing in Publication

Aitken, Kelley, 1954-, author
Canadian shield / Kelley Aitken.

Short stories.
ISBN 978-1-988040-09-7 (paperback)

I. Title.

PS8551.I776C36 2016 C813'.54 C2016-902235-8

This book is dedicated to Barbara Adelaide Bell Aitken, Elizabeth Flora MacLeod Hillier, and Fatemeh Iraji Akdari.

CONTENTS

THE WOUNDED BEAR

They're halfway to Hudson Bay on the Missinaibi, and this is Peterbell, a railroad stop. The name sounds attractive, even whimsical, a conflation of Peter Pan and Tinkerbell. Her kids had loved the book. Kay remembered her own eager faith, sitting in flannel PJs on the living-room carpet beside her brother and clapping like mad to prevent the fairy's light from disappearing.

But there's no whimsy here where the railroad crosses the river. Ugly cement stanchions rise out of the water, buttressing a span of track. In the grand or intimate scope of this river, they've passed through such beauty: walls of dark forest, sparkling water over rocks, and gold/green marshy flats. This is the first truly ugly place, a muddy pull-out beside a raw dirt cliff, abandoned rail cars and a clearing where felled trees are waiting to be chopped into firewood.

She's not sure she wants to disembark, but she says nothing because of her reputation: Mama Kay, always worrying. She wonders if worry is a function of aging, of parenting, or if, as a nurse, she has too often seen the bad effects of youthful exuberance and spontaneity, the sad and sometimes permanent outcome of not planning, not thinking, not listening.

There's a single cabin across the tracks. Kay can just see its roof beyond an old abandoned railcar. The others—her son Glen and his girlfriend Angie, her stepson Kevin—have already walked up the path. It's the usual state of affairs for Kay and Jack to be pulling up the rear. He wants his binoculars and can't find them. She straightens from rummaging around in the bottom of a pack in time to see a man emerge over the top of the knoll. She raises her hand diffidently, gives a little wave. For a full beat the man doesn't respond, and then, just as Kay is feeling the prickle of hair at the back of her neck, she sees the hand go toward the baseball cap and the brim dip in a gesture of hello. His arm drops, then he's gone.

By the time Kay and Jack have climbed the path, there he is again, with the others. Boyd is his name. Next to their tanned, healthy bodies his skin is sallow. The jeans he's wearing haven't seen a washing machine in a long time. Kay doesn't like the way his eyes linger on Angie's breasts.

"We're going inside," Glen gestures toward the cabin, "for *a cold drink*."

They've all tramped through the door under the rack of moose antlers and past the two rifles lying on a turquoise vinyl couch in the screened-in porch. After their eyes have adjusted to the dimly lit interior, they see, on every wall, glossy posters of young women, legs spread for the camera. "Snatch shots": she didn't know she knew the phrase. Kay is momentarily distracted by the caramel tones of the beauty nearest her and the wide vertical eye of her vagina, gaping at Kay as if returning her gaze. Kevin smirks from under his baseball cap.

Someone is seated at a table near an old wood-burning stove, someone whom Kay, trailing her taller companions, can't yet see. She steps out from behind Glen now to say hello and nearly bumps into Angie. Her pretty head is down, but she's blushing furiously and pushing to the back of the group. "Sorry dear," Kay says. Glen pats his mother on the shoulder as he turns to follow Angie, and Kay finds herself looking down at blue eyes in a bruised face.

The skin on one of the woman's cheekbones is abraded. Kay wants to press a cool cloth to that face, pinch open a Vitamin E capsule and rub gentle circles around those bruised and puffy eyes. Instead, she forces a smile. "Hot, isn't it?" she asks.

"Yup, sure is." The open collar of the woman's checked shirt reveals the pressed cleavage of middle age. Her hair is laced with grey, its original colour hard to guess, maybe light brown or dark blond but the yellowish sheen is nicotine. In the hospital, Kay would have asked, gently but firmly, "Who did this to you?" We could be the same age, she thinks.

"I'm Jean and this here's Wesley, my brother." He has a bandana tied like a skullcap over his head. The cut-off sleeves of his black t-shirt reveal tanned, muscular arms. Beside him is an overflowing ashtray. Jean is enjoying the attention; perhaps there aren't many, or any, mirrors out here. She casts her eyes over the group. "Any of you see the bear he shot this morning?"

"You shot a bear?" asks Kevin, eyes narrowing. Where Glen is tall and mellow, Kevin has the build and demeanour of a school-yard scrapper.

"Nicked him," says Wes, rocking back on the two legs of his wooden chair. "He ran into the woods. Let's hope he stays in there."

Kevin scowls.

Boyd leans against the counter. He tips his head back to drain his can of cola. All three of the cabin dwellers seem like children, bored in their playhouse.

"You got asthma?" Jean asks, directing her question toward Angie, poised at the door. She has just extracted an inhaler from her fanny pack.

"Well then," Jean says. She reaches over to take the just-lit cigarette out of her brother's mouth.

"What the ..." Wes says, surprised.

"There ya go," Jean says, proud of herself for creating the temporary no-smoking area in the otherwise haze-filled cabin.

Kay puts her pop can down on the counter. The sight of the dishes neatly laid out on a tea towel to dry is almost as alarming as the posters and the bruises on the woman's face.

"Thank you for the cold drink. Very refreshing," says Kay, "but we need to get back on the river."

"If I was you I wouldn't be in a rush to get to Thunder House," Wes says. He's talking about the famous, or infamous, waterfall. A few years back two teenaged boys were swept over it and drowned. The tragedy travelled like a virus through the paddling community.

"We're looking forward to seeing it," says Jack, the first words out of his mouth since he refused the beverage. "We'll eddy out and look at it from the bank, and then we'll do the portage."

Kay hears the belligerent edge in her husband's voice. She's nervous about the power of this river; they've passed a couple of wrecked canoes already.

"Didja see the smashed up canoe?" asks Wes, and it spooks her that her thoughts are somehow transparent.

He adds, "People die on this river every year."

But they took chances, Kay thinks, they either didn't bring a map or didn't use it well. People get into trouble when they misjudge the current or attempt a course they haven't the skill or strength to follow. She wants to leave but can't think of a way to muster the troops. She takes a step toward the door, almost reaching out her hand for the rest of them.

Jack's bold rudeness is enough to galvanize them. "Stuffy in here." He heads toward the door and suddenly everyone is on their feet and moving.

The sun is at its peak. Kay feels the accumulation of sweat under her breasts. The hot metal and creosote smell of the rails is welcome after the cabin's claustrophobic stink. A voice behind her says, "Don't step on that."

"On what?" she asks, alarmed as much by Boyd's proximity as whatever it is he's warning her about.

"That extra rail."

"Why not?" Though she knows her question has been scripted, like a knock-knock riddle.

"You'll be electrocuted," Boyd says.

Who's there? The electrocutioner. Electrocutioner who? But this isn't a joke and Boyd isn't funny. Yet, even in her discomfort, she recognizes the loneliness and boredom of this life. There's something deceptively earnest about them all. Kay is too polite and well-meaning to say the word stupid, even to herself. Instead she thinks *they're simple*, too far up a creek to know this isn't the way people behave. People like this show up at her hospital after the bars close, a handful each night. She stitches them up. Takes their temperature. Suggests bed rest and "plenty of fluids *but not alcohol*."

Right now she just wants to get back on the river. Her earlier eerie presentiment hasn't lifted. She finds herself thinking of that awful film *Deliverance*. Stepping carefully over the tracks, she picks up her pace. At the edge of the slope down to the canoes, she remembers her manners and turns to say goodbye to Boyd, only to discover she's alone; the others have stopped just beyond the tracks. Reluctantly, she walks back.

Kevin has dropped to one knee and is fiddling in the weeds. The rest are gathered around his broad shoulders, looking down. When Kay approaches he holds up his hand toward her, one finger pointing skyward, its tip coated in red.

She reacts, "Kevin, what happened?!"

"It's not my blood, it's the bear's."

Boyd sidles up to Kay and continues where he left off: "Didja see *Deliverance*?" he asks.

What's *with* these people?

"They filmed most of it around here," Boyd offers proudly. He says "fill-ummed," breaking the word into two syllables. "They wanted real bush."

"Well then," she says, "they came to the right place." She looks down at her husband crouched in the weeds beside his son. "Jack?"

But Jack isn't listening to her. "That bear needs to be trailed if it's badly hurt. You fellows planning to finish what you started?"

"Just nicked him," Wes says, again, glaring at Jack. In the stubborn set of her husband's shoulders, the grim line of his lips, Kay sees the horn-locking, what her son and stepson refer to, though with different emphasis, as "a guy thing."

"C'mon Jack," Glen says, laying his hand on the shoulder of his stepfather, "we've got a river waiting."

Later she will think how typically they all reacted—Kevin and Jack angry, ready to take offense; Glen mild, the eternal diplomat; Angie somehow apart, caught up in a miasma of insecurity; and Kay, mother hen, wanting to keep them all safe from harm, safe, even, from themselves.

Jack says, "I'll thank you to loan me a gun if you're not going to finish this yourself."

"Jack!" says Kay, turning to her husband in dismay.

"Be my guest," sneers Wes. "Think you can handle it?"

"Now, now," says Boyd, all diplomacy and fake heartiness. He takes off his stained cap and waves it around like a prop. "We don't need to worry about a li'l ol' bear."

"Sorry to disagree, pardner," this from Kevin and *why*, Kay wonders, *are they all talking like this is some Western*?

"That bear's losing a lot of blood. Gut shot, I'd imagine, or maybe a wound to the head."

How can the boy she's raised and the man she has slept beside, naked, for over two decades, know these things about blood and gunshots and wounds; how *can* they?

"You wanna indulge in a little blood sport," Wes says, "be my guest, but you can pay for the cartridges."

Now Boyd interjects. "We ain't givin' you the gun without some kind of insurance you're bringin' her back." He looks at Angie, lets his eye travel all the way down her tall frame. Instinctively, Kay steps between them, blocking his gaze.

"Leave the women here," he says, smirking at Kay and levelling his eyes at her chest. "As collateral."

Kay shivers with distaste but, as quickly, is relieved. That insult will get them all moving. She starts again to walk toward the river. At the brow of the slope she turns. Once again, she is alone. Jack and Kevin are heading back to the cabin with Wes. Kay feels the gall rising in her. This is too much. Glen's arm is wrapped around Angie's shoulders, his head bent towards her.

The men are behaving like "fucking cowboys." She has shocked herself with the expletive but not the sentiment. It's what one of her fellow nurses said recently, after a long night in emerg, adding, "Testosterone. I swear to God it's the stupidity hormone."

"They're pretending they want to put the bear out of its misery, but they just want to go hunting." This is from Glen, who has come down the path with Angie.

He lines up his hands as if holding a rifle and swings it three times from right to left.

"Bang," he says, pulling the imaginary trigger.

A shot echoes in the woods behind the cabin.

"Jesus! This place is spooky. Every time I think something, it happens or those guys say it or …"

"I know," says Kay. "I *know*."

"We're going to take a little paddle," Glen says. "Get some fresh air."

She would protest, *but you're already outside*, except that she understands her son's urge to clear off and wishes she could do the same.

"Boyd's gone with them," Glen says, answering her unasked question. "And that little gunshot seems to have been Wes showing Kevin how to fire one of the guns."

He slides his canoe back into the water, gets in and angles the bow back toward Angie so she won't have to get her feet wet. Kay is touched at these little acts of chivalry, but Jack and his son are inclined to scoff. In a not-so-quiet aside earlier in the day, Kevin had referred to Angie as "Miss Princess can't-take-the-piss."

Kay carries her sit-upon to a tree root and lowers herself to the ground. She fishes her book out of her bag. Except for the occasional whine of a mosquito, the air is still and hot. A raven flies over, and another, vocalizing, that *kerlunk* that sounds like a marble down a drain. The sky is bleached of colour. She doesn't know whether to be furious or glad that her men are thinking about that bear. The place gives her the creeps, but she has no choice except to wait.

She and Jack have been married for twenty-five years, the second time for each of them. Her first marriage was unconscious, hardly a choice; he was handsome and she got pregnant.

Even before she gave birth he was cheating on her, lying about their finances, borrowing against the house. She was falling out of love with him when she discovered she was pregnant again. It took five years to get up the gumption to leave. She rented a tiny flat and left the kids in the home they'd always known although she saw them every day, walking them back after school, cooking their dinner and then leaving as her husband came through the door. She never said a bad word about him, didn't want to poison the children's relationship with their father. It went on like that for months, and because it was that era, because by the luck of the draw their judge was a misogynist who painted her as a floozy for leaving the marital home, custody went to her ex. Kay felt that a light had been extinguished, and she imagined putting all her things in a backpack and travelling through Saharan Africa—not that the idea appealed, but an endless desert matched her state of mind. And then she met Jack. His wooing was diligent, even dogged. He was a hard-working advocate for wilderness parks and green politics. From evening picnics in the woods, they graduated to camping on weekends and holidays. It didn't erase her sadness, but her sorrow made more sense in natural surroundings. The rhythms somehow helped, the motion of her paddle in the water, setting up their tent and cooking dinner over a fire, and finally, Jack's tender ministrations between the puffed ridges of the sleeping bags.

An hour passes. Kay has taken off her sandals and is sitting in her canoe, feet out over the side. Her novel is open in her lap, but she can't concentrate on it. She's listening. Like an undercurrent to the silence and stillness, a flutter of sound, distant lapping. The bear? Drinking at the river? Suppose that by going into the woods they have actually forced it to double back. A twig snaps, immediately followed by a rasping sound. What was that? It might be trees rubbing together or an animal lumbering painfully, stopping to lean against the smooth trunk of a poplar, leaving a smear of red on pale green bark.

Kay, she warns herself.

The canoe comes around the bend under the railroad bridge: Glen and Angie, long arms moving in unison, paddling fast. Within moments they're bringing the bow into shore.

"What's wrong?" asks Kay.

Angie looks at Kay. "You didn't hear it?"

"What? Hear what?"

"Two shots and someone shouting," says Glen. "It didn't sound like Jack or Kevin."

He is already halfway up the path heading back in the direction where the men entered the woods. Kay steps into her sandals, adjusts Velcro.

Glen shouts at her, "Mom, come ON!"

At the tracks, they hear someone approaching, twigs snapping, a scuffle of feet in the leaf litter. Between the poplar and spruce trunks, the foliage is mottled with sunlight and shadow. Kay catches a glimpse of orange—it's Kevin. He's carrying the rifle, and his other arm is around Boyd's shoulders, propelling and pulling. "Kay," Kevin calls, and pushes Boyd forward. Kay and the others run to close the short distance.

Boyd's eyes are bloodshot and dazed. Above his right elbow, which he cradles as if it were a foreign object, the sleeve of his shirt is red. A drop of blood releases and hits the ground. Kay looks down, sees more blood on his shoe. She looks up again at his ashen face. A thin line of drool descends from his open lips.

"We need to elevate and clean that. Have you got a first-aid kit?" She asks stepping toward Boyd and steadying him on his uninjured side, her legs apart, braced.

"Angie, go get the first-aid kit."

"Sit down, Boyd." She gives his shoulder a gentle push. "Give him room," she snaps to the others. Boyd slumps to the ground. She peels his hat off and places her hand on the back of his head, pushing. "Head down," she says. "That's it." She takes her knife from her pocket, pinches the plaid cotton at Boyd's shoulder, inserts the blade and then rips down toward the wound. She lifts his hand and gently pries the blood-soaked cloth away.

"It doesn't look deep. Okay, let's keep the pressure on." She moves the bloody sleeve back into place and settles Boyd's hand over it again then places hers overtop of his. In triage you deal with the most acute case and then the next.

"Kevin, dear. Sit." Kay nods to Angie who steps forward and helps Kevin. Only when they're cross-legged in the leaf litter does Kay look around.

"Where's your father?!"

Kevin gives her a strange, almost sheepish look.

"*Tell* me!"

Jean and Wes arrive from the cabin. Jean, seeing Boyd, swears softly, takes a step toward him then backs away, "What happened?!"

"Kay." Her stepson is looking at her intently. There are blood beads on his forehead, a scratch probably, from an overhanging branch. "Dad's all right. He just needs a little time alone."

"What are you talking about?" She is rubbing slow circles on Boyd's back.

"It happened so fast. He shot … He did this, Kay." He points to Boyd's arm.

Wes guffaws, but his smile falls away.

Kevin continues as if he hasn't heard. "He took us by surprise in a little gully. The bear, I mean. Boyd had one gun and Dad had the other. The bear was shaking his head back and forth. There was a shot. When Boyd dropped the gun and went down, I thought he was … The bear went up on its hind legs, and I picked up the gun and fired and I …" his voice rises like an adolescent's, "*killed* it."

"Holy shit," whispers Glen.

Boyd is shivering.

"We need to get them both to the cabin," she says. "Glen, go and find Jack. Bring him back. He might be in shock."

Wes glares down at Kevin. "Unh, I *can* count, buddy. Where's the other gun?"

"He doesn't have it … He wasn't carrying it." Kevin swings his head around, looking back into the woods. "Shit, shit, shit."

Glen bends to place a hand on his stepbrother's shoulder. "I'll go."

"It's at the edge of the gully, near the … *bear*," Kevin's head drops to his knee.

"That's okay, Kev, I'll find it."

Back at the cabin, Kay asks for boiled water. Jean is opening cupboards, lighting the small gas stove, pulling clean tea towels out of a drawer. Long moments pass.

Kevin and Boyd are both settled into the two lower bunks. The whistle of the kettle pierces the quiet. Kay rises and crosses to the stove. She is back at Boyd's bunk and kneeling again, testing the heat of the cloth in the bowl of water beside her when Angie stands up abruptly.

"Hey," says Wes at the first sound of ripping paper. Jean turns from the sink. Now all of them are staring as Angie pulls a centrefold from the wall.

Wes tries again. "What do you think you're doing?" But the question is nervous, as if even he senses that Angie mustn't be provoked.

"I …" says Angie, her voice half way between groan and growl.

"have …"

"had …" she is making her way around the stuffy room. The swift rasp of tearing paper punctuates her words.

"… enough!"

There are two pink spots of colour on her cheeks. Kay thinks she has never seen the young woman look so beautiful, too bad Glen's in the woods. But maybe it's because he isn't here, isn't protecting or running interference for her. Angie rips the last poster down and holds the crumpled ball in both hands, momentarily stymied, then strides to the woodstove. She yanks the metal door open, shoves in the wad of paper and paws through her pouch. Just as Kay is wondering if she needs her inhaler, Angie pulls out a lighter.

Jean, coming over from the sink, opens the damper. She smiles at Angie, gives her a quick double pat on the back.

Wes scrapes back his chair and goes outside.

Jean kneels beside Kay. "Is he gonna be all right?" Jean asks.

Kay finishes taping gauze over Boyd's wound. "I think so, but you should take him to a clinic, get it checked out."

"We can flag down a freight train and go to Foleyet. Wes won't have to come." She says the last bit under her breath. "He isn't my brother, Kay, he's my son, but he's ashamed that he still lives with me."

"But are you okay?" Kay asks.

"Oh me," Jean shrugs. "Day I can't handle myself with these two is the day I leave." She takes the bowl of bloody water and cloths to the sink.

Kay hears Glen outside. Wes bangs in through the screen door and leans the rifle against the wall. As soon as Glen enters the cabin, Angie takes his hand and pulls him outside.

Kevin throws off the sleeping bag and sits up. "Let's go."

"Are you sure you're all right?" Kay asks.

"Don't baby me," he snaps. And then, "Sorry, Kay, I'll be fine once we get going."

Jean strips blankets from the other bunks and lays them gently on Boyd. Kay leaves her clean dressings and tape and then, impulsively, hugs Jean, "You take care of yourself," she says, conscious of tears at the back of her throat.

Heading down the path to the water, Kay sees Jack, seated on her tree root, his head in his hands. When she approaches he moves over to the canoe and starts fussing with their gear. He directs his question at a dry bag. "Is Boyd okay?"

Kay sighs and answers. "It's just a flesh wound."

Their departure is swift, the three canoes in single file, passing under the railroad bridge, leaving it behind as if there are two parallel lines on this mysterious river, as if it is booby-trapped beyond these imaginary borders. After what seems about an hour of paddling, Kay looks at her watch. It's almost five. But at the first campsite, Kevin demurs. "Let's keep going for a while."

An hour later they're setting up camp on the east side of the river. It is as lovely as Peterbell was bleak, a sloping skirt of granite levelling off to a flat area partly embraced by a hemlock grove. The sun sends long shadows across the site, and a welcome breeze has come up; it wards off most of the bugs. Kay breaks out the scotch and pours it into five cups. Even Angie drinks hers.

After a simple dinner and far earlier than usual, everyone says goodnight, anxious for this day to be over.

In the tent Jack turns to her. She takes him in her arms. He shudders and burrows his head into her neck. So softly that she almost doesn't hear it, he says, "I'm sorry." If she let him, they'd make love, but other than motherly pats on his back, she can't comfort him, not tonight.

Up early, Kay bathes nude in the river, her morning ritual unless its raining. She washes her hair and then leans backward to rinse it, shaking her head from side to side. On shore again, she dries herself off, donning her t-shirt and undies, sitting on her towel to smooth cream into her legs. The sun has just grazed the tip of the tallest pines, and the sky itself is shifting from blush to lemon. "Oh sweet Canada Canada Canada," sings the white-throated sparrow. The zip of a tent door means someone else is awake.

Angie walks down to the water, steps down onto the underwater ledge Kay just vacated and dives. Unlike Kay, she is wearing a swimsuit. She resurfaces a few metres out, then tucks and bottoms up like a duck. After her feet disappear she pops up again, hair slick to her scalp. She swims quick lengths back and forth and then swims back to shore and gets out. She dries off then lays her towel flat on the ground beside Kay.

Sensing that the young woman needs something, Kay pats her arm. "That was a good thing you did yesterday."

Angie says nothing for a while, then stands and gathers her towel.

"Thanks, Mama Kay," she says before walking away.

Kay's cheeks burn though her body is cool. She is stepping into her pants when she sees Glen coming toward her from the other side of the rock.

He waits until he is beside her then nudges her arm and points. Further down on the opposite bank a moose grazes, unaware of their presence. As they watch, it moves off, trotting from one marshy island to another, through arrowheads and pickerelweed and into a short stretch of open water. He's either playing or trying to get rid of his attendant cloud of insects, bending and then rearing his head in bouncy sequence with a high-stepping gait.

"Mom," he says, "I have to tell you, there was no bear."

"What?"

"Kevin says he killed it but there was nothing there. No dead bear."

"Maybe you missed it, maybe it fell into the gully."

"I don't think so. Even if it was somehow down a slope or behind a bush, I'd have heard the flies, the sound would have lead me to it. No flies, other than the few that were bothering me. I think Wes was right, he just nicked him."

"Why didn't you say something, before they went off?"

"Mom, Jack and Kevin *don't* listen to me as a rule. I figured they'd get their adrenalin rush and come back empty handed. But by the same token, if the bear was hurt? It was a hard call." He tosses more pebbles, one at a time, into the water."When you're a kid, the first time you shoot a rifle, you think you've blown away the world."

"When did you shoot a rifle?" she asks in alarm. "Did your father take you hunting?"

"Mom, calm down. Jack took us to a rifle range. We didn't tell you because ..." he gives her a quick grimace.

"I'd have worried." She sighs.

"Actually, I was better than Kev. He assumes he hit the bear because, well, guns do that to people. They were hot and psyched and they came upon the bear—or maybe they just thought they did—and in the excitement Boyd got in Jack's line of fire.

"But at the first shot, the bear would have run away. He's not going to stand around waiting. I heard the rifle go off. Twice. There was a long pause in between. Angie heard the same thing."

Kay looks at her son.

Glen continues, "Did Boyd say something different?"

"No. He was in shock, he *wouldn't* know."

"What did Jack say?"

"That he was sorry. After he shot Boyd, I don't imagine he was aware of anything else. Mom, the bear's still out there."

Kay emits a short groan.

"Listen, we're heading out of the area, and we already take all sorts of precautions, hanging up the food, wearing whistles on portages. We can't quit the trip now, unless you want to go back to Peterbell and wait for a passenger train."

"God, no."

"I don't think we'll run into it," he looks directly at her. "He's gun shy. But I don't want to get everyone all excited again."

"You have to tell Kevin, at least," Kay says. "Whatever he felt when he was holding that gun, it's not how he feels now."

That day and the next she watches the shoreline so carefully that Jack snaps at her, "Relax for Christ's sake!" After Glen takes Kevin aside—she doesn't in fact witness this but can tell by Kevin's mood—he isn't as scrappy as he was earlier. Even Angie seems more at home in her skin.

The river widens after the falls, becomes gravelly, a foot or two of fast flowing water over rock gardens and pebble bars; sometimes the rapids don't let up, they're as much as a kilometre long. They're enjoying themselves, and the memory of Peterbell fades behind them. But sometimes, alone on a portage trail, a pack on her back, another smaller one hanging over her tummy, Kay imagines she hears the snapping twigs, the sounds of breathing or the soft padding of feet on forest floor that mean it's coming. *Maybe belief was enough to save something.* She pauses and looks toward the sound.

And then fear blooms in her stomach and she starts walking again, as fast as her load will allow, making noise, fumbling the whistle into her mouth, blowing short wispy breaths into it and clapping her hands to scare what is or isn't there, and at the end of their last portage with sunlight sparkling on the lake ahead, the sound of her two sweaty hands coming together makes her remember.

"Tinkerbell," she says aloud.

Hunter

They are downwind of the heron. It doesn't see them until the nose of the canoe snags a lily, the waxy yellow flower dipping first in one direction then another, like a buoy tugged by an underwater swimmer. She has been leaning to the right of the bow, watching as its silky forward thrust displaces lily pads and parts their waving stems. In fact she doesn't see the bird until it flies a short distance, settles in reeds and, again, presumes invisibility.

Their progress downriver has disturbed ducks, whole families pedaling furiously, the mother veering off and sometimes faking a broken wing. The incapacity of the birds to suss out the situation, their logic, or lack of it, amuses her and makes her feel guilty at the same time. She feels herself a monster then, potent and inexorable, pushing onward, pushing fear into what was tranquil air above this tranquil water.

"We see you," she whispers to the heron. "We mean you no harm." But a few heavy beats of those big wings carry it up into a white pine. It looks Dr Seuss-ish. So do their communal nurseries, loose nests in stands of dead timber, dozens of them, like floppy straw hats.

When the heron pushes off the branch, its flapping is so slow and weighted it seems impossible it could be airborne, but there—it is. Then that prehistoric retraction of the neck. She tucks in her own chin instinctively and thinks of what her esophagus looks like, a flattened section of inner tube, a garden hose lifted, folded, and squeezed in the sprinkler games they played as children; thinks of Belle, the air choked out of her—the one bad choice snowballing, a relentless propulsion of obsession and guilt, and how afterward her fate could be traced like the forward momentum of panicked ducklings, a narrowing wake of harbingers in a previously calm and happy life.

At her death Belle was wearing a pair of dangling gold earrings. Neither her fiancé, Mac, who identified the body nor her roommate, Helen, recognized them. And, it was explained, in the sense that anything was "explained" by the inquest, that a blown up photograph of Belle taped to Paul's wall bore two piercings, slightly larger than a pinhole, through the earlobes. Paul had apparently given them to the picture first.

The heron is far away, its art-nouveau silhouette now just another speck on the horizon. Cam steers the canoe across the river. "Smartweed," he says. She looks for a tiny upright cluster, bright pink.

Cameron hadn't been bothered by Anna's aura of grief. He was never an ardent suitor. The first time he used the word love, it floored her. They were in Ottawa for a weekend. "Let me introduce you to our nation's capital," he'd said, and so they'd driven up, toured the National Gallery and Parliament buildings, and visited his friends. Before the drive home on Sunday, he suggested a walk by the river. Others had been there before them, piling rock figures on its gravelly shore. Cam began to build one. She looked out over the grey-green water, feeling the presence of his ex-wife in this city he knew so well. He was lifting a large piece of granite to lay crossways on two smaller uprights when she blurted out, "Do you think of her?" He turned his head toward her and said, "Don't you know I love you, Anna?" She held her breath, their future suddenly bound in the balance of three uneven rocks. But he was good with his hands, he'd wiggled the granite into its precarious cradle and lifted his palms away slowly, long fingers still curved, as if by sheer force of will he'd make it stay. It did. Only then did he walk to Anna and fold her in a hug.

Love. His for her was steady. Reliable. She hadn't known what she felt, at the start—her own need, probably, for something and someone to hold on to, this lithe man behind her in the canoe. His presence in her life went partway to filling the hollow carved out by Belle's death. She refused to say "vacuum," although that is what it was. She couldn't handle one either and resorted to a dust-buster to clean her throw rugs. It wasn't the only word excised from her vocabulary. She avoided "stalk," even when used to indicate part of a plant, and "choke," which had, of late, come into common usage as a way to suggest a sudden loss of confidence.

To say those words was to let in the howling darkness. Cam, too, had experienced loss, the death of a younger brother in a sky-diving accident. Cam said he figured everything was fine until Trevor was just shy of his target, a fallow square of farmland between county roads. But he was a first-time parachute—"first-and-last-time," Cam said—and though he aimed for the field he came down spread-eagled on hydro wires, and the force of his descent was enough to rip them from their housings."The minute he hit the ground, he was the connection. Blew the bottom off his shoes and pretty much fried him."

Cam could say "wire" and "hydro," even "electrocution," and he'd jumped out of a plane himself although he kept that from his mother, because, as he explained with yet another phrase Anna couldn't use, "She'd have killed me."

"I didn't want Trevor's death to make me, you know, carry that fear around."

She knew he didn't mean to compare. He accepted her grief and superstitions. They had their matched losses, a sibling each.

Underway again, the stroking of paddles the only discernible motion around, she daydreams. Cam was right not to let losses define his life. He knew when to cut them. Did she? Her mind drifts back to last week's echocardiogram, to the small darkened cubicle at the medical arts centre.

The technician squirted clear jelly beside Anna's left breast. Next came the hard, smooth whatsits moving in arcs over her skin. The computer screen was positioned so that Anna couldn't see what for her would be unreadable anyway, the squiggles and ghostly shapes reflected as vague blue flickers on the pretty technician's face. "The four horsemen of the apocalypse"—that phrase and a clear but anachronistic mental picture popped into her head when she heard, through the computer's speakers, the wet clotty sound of her heart, like horses on a muddy road, lugubrious and yet comforting. If one horse fell through the hole—she was convinced there was a hole in her heart—there were still three to keep the blood pushing through her veins.

But there was no hole, just a tiny flap that was sluggish on the uptake, a "mitral-valve prolapse." She might need to take precautionary antibiotics prior to dental work or a minuscule chip of plaque could enter her bloodstream and travel into her heart through that half-open door. A friend of hers had a brother-in-law who'd died that way. Or a friend's friend? It verged on the apocryphal, like stories from the Reader's Digest, traded over coffee with a workmate and, later, in the squishy way of memory, attributed to a relative or acquaintance. Even with six degrees of separation, was it possible that everyone knew someone else whose brother, mother, or second-cousin's girlfriend had died in some peculiar way? Belle's story was just such a magnet, a source—real, historical—for the blossoming of legend in the minds of others. Not for Anna's or Cam's friends and families, but the people who knew the people who knew them, and all the waves and ripples of people beyond that, so that often Anna felt uneasy with new acquaintances, leery of what she imagined was a prurient curiosity, "Isn't she the one with the sister who …"

She, Anna thinks, is the place in me that things slip through. Things like Cam's recent marital lapse, the one she wasn't meant to know about. Here was a man who'd jumped out of a plane six months after his brother's sky-diving death to see what it felt like to hurtle through miles of blue sky. A man who might take a lover to better understand what had propelled his partner toward infidelity.

Maybe the valve in her heart wasn't just sluggish, maybe it didn't close well enough to keep her man in, to keep what they had safe. Knowing about his infidelity made her understand, that he, finally, had been aware of hers.

Anna had delayed doing anything with her sister's ashes, partly because the idea of spreading them in the foothills of the Rockies, the same area where Belle had been taken to die, was too painful. In the wake of that death, Anna felt guilty for breathing.

What motivation she could muster was spent in fierce memory, to keep her sister's spirit alive. She never felt that Paul's suicide atoned for what he'd done; she hated him for his cowardice, his own death too easy, too much an act of avoidance. Her mother, a brittle diabetic, died within two years of the incomprehensible murder of her oldest child, grief paving the way for a fatal heart attack. A few years later, Anna's father sold the Scarborough bungalow and moved in with the woman he would take as his second wife, into a bustling split-level, full, on weekends and at family holidays, of grandchildren and the smell of roasting meat. Anna peeled potatoes and patted the children's heads, but this was another family's ritual.

Perhaps it was a sense of life's brevity that prompted Helen to marry shortly after the inquest. And though Mac had mourned deeply, he, too, found a partner, Kay, with whom he now had two children. People did this; they moved on. But Anna lived surrounded by the physical remnants of her childhood, furnishings her father hadn't taken when he remarried. He'd helped Anna move, helped her to finance her small Toronto townhouse. There, the blue sofa and armchair, the dark wooden table and Royal Doulton dishes gave off echoes of her youth. She had, she suspected, become one of those melancholic single women. Old friends fell away. Men felt the vibes and steered clear.

Until Cam. He seemed to take for granted that she'd be a part of his own unhurried future.

And so a year almost to the day of his Ottawa River declaration, eight years after her sister's death, Anna took the urn down from a high shelf in the cupboard and booked a flight west. What she feared if she looked again at those craggy peaks and deep valleys—the yawning pit of grief and horror—would be manageable because she'd be coming home to Cam.

Mac met her in Calgary. That night, Anna went through boxes in his basement, boxes he'd packed and stored—for eight years!—because she'd been too upset to deal with the clothes and books and knick-knacks.

In the third carton, she found her sister's hiking gear: backpack, anorak, and a knife, not the Swiss Army version she might have expected, but a bone-handled blade in a leather sheath. There were boots, too, stiff with disuse. Belle had forced Anna to buy a pair, had rattled on with the staff person in the outdoor store about half and three-quarters shank. Anna rolled her eyes.

"Can't I just wear my runners?"

"You do that and you'll never go hiking again," Belle said. "Good boots make all the difference."

But good boots hadn't saved her from Paul.

On the trail, Anna hiked behind Mac. In choosing him, her sister had found the antithesis to burly, bearded Paul. Mac was balding and slight, even slightly elfin, with an almost handsome face. By mid-afternoon, they'd reached the high ledge where he proposed they camp. It took a few minutes to set up camp, and they were ascending again, aiming for a higher ledge and "one of Belle's favourite views."

At the lookout they stood without speaking, the silence punctuated by the cawing of distant crows and Anna's ragged breaths, her Toronto lungs unused to the altitude. Before them, the bowl of valley embraced a river. Steadfast pines rose straight from their steep footing and the bare rock above the tree line seemed receptive as flesh in the pinkening light.

"She loved this time of day," Mac said. "She used to say we'd earned our rest."

"Maybe we ought to say something," Anna started, but no, his smile made her see it wasn't necessary. The woman they'd come to honour was present in every reaching branch, in the thrust and drop of land and the river below.

They unscrewed the urn and took turns tossing handfuls over the edge. The ashes fluttered and drifted in the slight breeze. Some settled against the steep rocky incline. Some were lifted and travelled almost as far as the trees. Rain, wind, and gravity would aid their dispersal. For a moment Anna pictured a diagram from elementary school, "The Water Cycle": wiggly arrows seeping into the earth while others swept down the mountain and into a turquoise ocean, up again into plump clouds. She could feel the land taking on the burden she had carried. So simple, this ritual, nature taking back what it had never really given up.

It was late afternoon, a veil of shadow pushed inexorably up the golden eastern slope of the valley. They sat with their feet over the edge until Mac slung his arm over her shoulder. "If we want light to cook in …" After dinner they built a small fire. As its smoke drifted up to the stars, they talked, quietly, about Belle.

When Anna woke in the dark, she unzipped her sleeping bag and Mac's and curled into him from behind, spooning. He turned. The velvet night and the land conspired, encasing them. Anna tucked her head into his neck and pulled him over on top of her. As he raised himself above her he said "Belle." When it was over, she held him to her chest. Tears spilled down her temples while his sperm trickled between her legs, and she saw again those textbook arrows, wiggling into the earth and rock beneath them. The Water Cycle.

In the morning, she waited till he rose and left the tent. Her head was spinning, a dozen rabbity thoughts: What did it mean? How could she tell Cam? And then the flush of remembered pleasure. Her hand swept across her pubis. It shocked her to know she'd do it again. She crawled out of the tent, kept her eyes on the ground until she could stand and turn toward the distant ridge. She could hear Mac walking up behind her. She felt one hand on her shoulder and saw the other as it wove into view, fingers gripping the handle of a coffee cup.

She took the cup, brought it to her lips, sipped and finally looked at him.

"Anna," he stopped and blew out a long stream of air. "It's this thing we've carried. Or held." As his voice faded—failing him?—his fingers closed and opened. It struck her then that, more than anything, the way a man uses his hands defines his character to the world. His would always cherish what they had held, even as they came up empty now, grasping at air. She saw that it was her turn—a novel feeling—to offer reassurance out of the abundance and sadness they had brought up into the foothills.

"For Belle." As soon as she said it, she knew that was how they'd leave it, never mind that a part of her wanted to crawl right back into last night's embrace. And only then did she feel the rest of her life reaching for her from over a mountainous skyline; she was picturing Cam as she'd last seen him, the airport hug that pressed her nose into the button of his shirt.

One of those odd, indelible details from the inquest: unwashed but folded neatly and placed under the pillow on his bed, a pair of women's underwear, plain cotton, from The Bay. The rest of the apartment a ramshackle mess, dirty dishes on the counter, beer bottles used as ashtrays, muddy boots, tool chest spilling its contents by the door, clothes in a pile at the bottom of the closet, old newspapers and a recent *Penthouse*.

A vacuum, missing its hose.

The pierced photo taped to the wall.

Man stalks ex-girlfriend, abducts and kills her, then kills himself.

Had he suggested a hike to Anna? A walk in the bush, and did she go along with him because she thought one more talk would ease his pain at her rejection? She must at least have been willing to go for a drive. The autopsy ruled out drugs. Belle was no mere slip of a girl, she must have fought back, but it didn't matter "how" anymore, the end result was the same. Strangled her a half a mile down an old logging road in the Kananaskis, cleared of snow by a recent chinook. And when that was done he attached a vacuum hose—he'd come prepared—to the exhaust and fed it through the car's undercarriage and up under the backseat, popping off one of the cushions, duct tape to secure it. Got back in the driver's seat and started the car, waiting for death beside his ex-girlfriend, whose head he'd arranged so that it faced away from him, appalled, perhaps, by the effects of strangulation on that beautiful face.

A fresh snowfall a few days later brought cross-country skiers to the road, who found the car and saw the bodies in it.

Anna has played the what-if game more times than she can count in the thirteen years since her sister's murder. What if there'd been no chinook, the warm and wind-borne breath of the Pacific sliding down the eastern slopes of the Rockies, what if the road hadn't been passable, what if Mac hadn't been called to a veterinary emergency, what if Belle had heeded warnings. What if the portent of Anna's dream, the night before the abduction, had propelled her onto the red-eye to Calgary? What if Belle, fearless funny Belle, hadn't opened the door to Paul that long ago Friday night.

Anna met Paul only once, a year after her sister had ended the relationship. Anna was in Calgary for the Stampede, had flown out using Belle's points, a graduation gift from elder to younger sister on her recent completion of library school. She'd spent the day sightseeing while Belle was at work. Then, as she turned off the sidewalk and cut across the lawn, the screen door opened and a man came out of her sister's house. The door banged, opened again for Belle. She introduced them, but he avoided Anna's eye. There was an awkward silence. Excusing herself, Anna went inside. Coming out of the washroom a few minutes later she thought she heard an odd sound, almost a yelp from outside, then the sound of scuffling, then nothing. Even as she reasoned with herself, *front porch, broad daylight,* Anna was hurrying back toward the door. Through the screen, over Belle's shoulder, Anna intercepted his gaze, and—in the only look they ever exchanged—understood what losing her sister had meant to this man. It wasn't malice or even jealousy. No, the bleak light in his eyes was both more and less than that, hunter and hunted in one. And then he moved, taking two of the porch steps at a time, a lumbering animal in retreat.

For years after the murder, that brief meeting spawned a recurring nightmare.

In the dream, as in life, Belle turns to her, a look of misery on her face. But the dream-Anna steps out onto the porch as a pair of bear-like paws close around her sister's throat. Man or monster?—it only matters that there is a danger to Belle. Anna rushes forward. She would pummel him with her fists! But he's gone. "Look, Belle," she says, and it is always like this, the moment of reprieve and elation, "I scared him away." Turning, she sees no-one, her sister, too, has disappeared.

It was Mac who identified the body, but Anna has always been haunted by what she didn't see. A victim of strangulation is no Pre-Raphaelite Ophelia, drifting downstream with the water lilies.

For the police it was over: the murderer known and furthermore, dead. It was hardly a new story: *If I can't have you in life* ... but it didn't stop there for Anna. She wanted more from the inquest than creepy facts exhaled by a shabbily furnished flat. It wasn't the one memory she had of Paul, those hunted eyes, his back as he crossed the lawn towards his car. It wasn't even his doppelganger, the bear-like creature of her dreams. No, what plagued her was that part of Belle unknown to her survivors, the part that had responded to a difficult and ultimately violent man.

She and her sister were in the habit of long calls on weekends. In the months after she'd met Paul, Belle had described picnics and hikes, then camping trips.

"He's a little rough around the edges, but I don't mind that."

"A man's man?"

"You could say that."Though also "moody," even, on occasion "volatile." But Belle liked the way he talked about the land, the way he knew it. He'd spent a lot of time in the woods as a kid. She and Paul often hiked in Kananaskis.

"How's Paul?" Anna asked one weekend. Her sister had stopped describing camping trips.

"We're taking a break." No explanation.

Anna blithered to fill in the silence, gossip about her classes and questions about Belle's veterinary clinic.

Weeks passed.

"We're just not compatible, emotionally," Belle said, when Anna asked again. And then, in a tone that indicated she wouldn't elaborate, "or physically."

Impotence. Kinky stuff. Date rape? Even between sisters some things would not be shared. At some point Belle began to talk about Mac.

It was summertime again when Belle suggested that Anna fly out after her graduation. Belle brought her new boyfriend to the airport, and the three of them went to dinner. Mac was smart, relaxed with himself, solicitous towards Anna. She felt at ease in the glow around them.

Then the next day there was that incident on the porch. After Paul left, Belle had remained where she was. Standing just inside the screen door, Anna wanted to ask something, anything: *Are you okay? What was that about? Are you still seeing him?* But her sister's stillness was a reproach. Anna backed away.

Coming downstairs after her shower, she accepted the proffered glass of wine. Yellow plates and a vase of garden flowers on a garden table bathed in summer light. The agenda for the weekend included a hike with Mac, but tonight it was just the two of them, a quiet celebration. As her sister served barbequed chicken and salad, Anna blurted, "Did you wash your hands?" Because who knew where Belle's hands had been that day, up the yahoo of some cow, emptying a vat of mare's urine, squeezing the testicles of a bull.

Belle wiggled long fingers under Anna's nose and tucked into her own cooking.

"So? What was that about?"

Belle looked out the window "He just wanted to drop something off."

"Like a bad mood?"

Belle's eyes gave off a warning. "He goes for week-long tramps in the bush and just likes to check in with someone on the way home."

"That's checking in?"

Belle ignored the question. "Sometimes he brings me back stuff." She pointed to the windowsill: eagle feathers, bones, and a small bird's nest. "Stuff he finds."

"Or hunts?"

"He used to do that, yes."

"Are you trying to 'cure' him?"

"I 'cure' animals, where and when I can." Belle put her fork down. "I assume you like Mac."

"Mac? Yes! A lot, actually. I'm happy for ..."

Belle interrupted. "Then why fixate on someone I'm not going out with anymore."

"Does *he* know that?"

"Is this schoolgirl jealousy, Anna? Because he's taken a tiny bit of my attention on your visit?"

Anna flushed and wanted to protest, but the grim set to her sister's jaw kept her silent. Later, getting ready for bed, Anna brooded. She had no practice at looking out for another's welfare. And maybe that's all Belle was doing—seeing a kinship, perhaps, between Paul and some of the creatures that found their way to the clinic. Gentling him like she did the horses and cattle she doctored on ranches bordering the city.

But in the months and years after the murder, Anna berated herself. If the situation had been reversed, wouldn't Belle have moved heaven and earth to protect her younger sister? At the first sign of resistance, Anna had backed down. Had her own needs—to maintain the familiar dynamic, to distance herself from the charge of jealousy—contributed to her sister's death?

Back in Ontario, after the ash scattering ceremony in the mountains, Anna avoided sex with Cam. She pleaded fatigue the night he met her flight and general malaise in the days that followed. But what started as a fib morphed into real symptoms. She was home with a bad cold the morning the Fed Ex truck stopped outside her door. Walking back down her hallway, she tore open the envelope and extracted its contents, a sheet of copy paper folded around several notebook pages.

Mac wrote, "I took one of Belle's old anatomy books off the shelf last night. This fell out. I started to read it. It seems to be a letter or a journal entry, and it's clear that the man is Paul. Call when you've read it."

Anna placed a pot of tea on the old kitchen table she'd eaten at as a child. She poured a cup, added lemon and honey, and unfolded the pages.

He came back to the tent just as I was boiling the water for coffee. I was bent over the stove, fiddling with the gauge. He came up behind me. I started to turn and—I remember this quite clearly—I hadn't looked at him in the face yet, because of my position, but I did notice that there was a stain on his jeans, near the knee, it looked wet but not like water, and now, looking back, I realize it was my last, what shall I call it: my last untainted act or observation, noticing and wondering about that stain. His hands came over my eyes then, the way someone does when they're going to give you a present. I let myself be led to the tent and pushed—gently—down on the sleeping bags. "Can I look," I asked? In reply, he made a little noise, "nh nh." I kept my eyes closed. He unbuttoned my blouse, unzipped and pulled off my shorts and underwear. I heard him unzip his pants, the rustle of cloth as he wriggled out of them. His lips were everywhere, and in the warm air those spots where he'd kissed were like tiny cool oases, on my breasts, belly, thighs, and then his tongue inside me. I felt myself sink into that lovely place; he'd never gone down on me before though I'd more or less suggested it at least a half dozen times. His fingers splayed across my skin, traced circles around my nipples.

He'd come back with the smells of the woods on him, and now, with my eyes closed, the odour on him reminded me of something almost disquieting, but that thought dissolved in my pleasure. I was listening to the sounds we made: the little slurps and moans, the movement of skin against the nylon of the sleeping bags and tent. It was unlike all the other times before. He entered me. At first, I was matching his rhythm, ready to slip over the edge, almost there … And then suddenly it was that kind of fucking. The kind that didn't include me.

"Slow down," I whispered. "Be soft." But he was possessed by it and as he raised himself above me, still slamming into his orgasm—mine had evaporated with his roughness—I opened my eyes. And I saw it all over his face, I saw it all across my body, what I'd taken for sweat or the moisture of his lips and tongue, but it was neither. I knocked him off me then and scrambled out of the tent and I was swatting at my skin, trying to erase the kisses that led from my chest to my pubic hair and down my thighs. All that blood. I reached between my thighs and my hand came out pink and slick, a mix of come and blood.

I was beside myself. I ran to the stream, grazed my ankle as I slipped, more blood, God, it was ridiculous. I suddenly worried that some other camper might come down the path. I went down on all fours, splashing and scrubbing. He'd traced circles around the aureoles of my nipples, and for a second I saw what he'd seen: leering bullseyes. It freaked me out.

I knew it wasn't mine; my period was over by a week. I never bleed between. Where had he gone and what had he done to get the blood? Was it his? But my hands had roamed his body; I hadn't felt a cut, and there was so much; I mean, a LOT.

His knife. It had never occurred to me to think of it as a weapon; knives are just a part of camping gear. He'd risen early—I'm always in admiration of that, how he can't get enough of the woods, like he doesn't want to miss a minute of it, certainly not the morning birds, the possibility of seeing a bear or an elk coming to drink at the water's edge. I'd always assumed that those early walks of his were filled with bird-watching and listening, something appreciative and benign …

But the blood on me had to have come from something, an animal in the woods that he'd tracked down, or worse, trapped. He'd walked into the trees while I'd put up the tent the afternoon before—to set a snare?

The sun hadn't yet reached the creek. Our campsite was set back off the trail but even now, clean, I was shivering, suddenly horrified at what I, in a sexual fog, had unwittingly condoned. Had he brought me here to do that? And how had he carried the blood back to the tent? When he took me into the tent, laid me down on the sleeping bags, he hadn't said a word. Why?

Because the blood had come back in the only "container" he had, his mouth.

A small sound formed in Anna's throat. She stood abruptly and walked to the sink, gagging. There was a metallic taste in her mouth. Water. She filled a glass, brought it to her lips and swooshed water around behind her teeth. She spit this into the sink. She filled the glass again and drank it down. She was breathing like a bull, like a prize fighter. In his *mouth,* but also in Belle's *body* …

"Don't do this to me," Anna said, slamming her hand against the counter. She felt as if she had just vomited, that reamed-out, burnt-nostril feeling. How had Belle managed to keep interacting with him? Anna wiped her face on the towel hanging over the handle of the oven door. She walked back to the table and picked up the notebook pages.

He was still in there. I stood outside, and I was feeling, I don't know, shame, anger. I stood there, covering my breasts and privates with my hands.

Privates—a little-girl word.

"Paul, you have to come out."

The nylon moved, but he didn't emerge.

"Come out. Now. I need my clothes."

I knelt in front of the door. Through the mosquito netting I could see him seated cross-legged on the sleeping bags. He had the hunting knife in one hand, the blade of it resting on his wrist. Tears were streaming down his cheeks, muddying the warrior stripes. He was still naked.

There was a quick stinging pinch on my bum, a late season mosquito. I slapped it and said "Damn!" Or something like that. His eyes flew up to meet mine through the screen. I could see he was upset, I mean, he was like a little boy. And though earlier I'd had a moment of fear, I could see there was no danger. I could see that.

"Go wash." It was weird; I was speaking to him in the same voice I use with the cows when they're nervous, the purebred dogs. "Go down to the stream." He came out of the tent on all fours, the knife still gripped in his right fist.

"Give me the knife, Paul," I said.

This line coincided with the end of a page. Anna slid this beneath the small pile in front of her. But on the next, she read, again: *He came back to the tent just as I …*

It was the first page.

"Oh Belle, don't stop. Don't leave me hanging." Too late, Anna realized she'd broken her taboo. The image of blood on skin morphed into the nightmare mask, bulging eyes and protruding tongue. Like a drunk, she grabbed for the phone. She dialed.

Kay answered.

Anna hung up.

In the memory of making love to Mac, Anna had seen herself as vessel, Belle's spirit rising through rock and earth, Mac reaching for them both, the lover he mourned and her living sister. Yes, Anna had slept in Kay's house after the overnight trip with Mac, had hugged her goodbye before going to the airport, but that was before Kay knew. Mac was that kind of man; he'd tell his partner the truth. That single "Hello?" had reduced what had happened between Anna and Mac to its simplest terms. Adultery.

She called Cam.

Tribal, it was the word he used later that evening, after he'd read the story, after she'd scrambled some eggs and made toast, brought it to him on a tray and then, remarking that she was "still contagious," seated herself across the room from him.

"When we were kids, Trevor and I cut ourselves," he put down his fork and swiveled one thumb against the other. "Blood brothers."

"But you were already related."

"Kids want magic. We had a secret society, too. A club house. Weekly passwords." He smiled.

"Did you kill animals and smear their blood on your bodies?"

"No, but we did shoot at the odd squirrel with our pellet guns."

"This is different," she said.

"Yes and no. You're thinking of him as a killer, here," he tapped the story in his lap. "But he wasn't there yet, I mean, I think this contributed. Her disapproval ..."

"How else should she have responded? My God, Cam, are you defending him?!"

"No! But this happened well before your sister was killed. You've got this loner, an odd, solitary guy. And he meets this beautiful woman. She's capable and warm and even interested in him."

Anna shook her head. "That's the part that stuns me."

"It stunned him, too. At some level he knew he didn't stand a chance."

"So why push it? Why do something so grotesque?"

"I'll bet you, Anna, he didn't mean it to be as weird as it ended up. He was just operating on that level, like Trevor and I when we were kids. Symbolic behavior. We all practice it."

She couldn't meet his gaze. Had he guessed about her and Mac?

"This is when your sister breaks off the intimate relationship. Maybe she had other reservations; we'll never know. But he starts to spiral into depression or desperation. Anna, your sister's murder was terrible, horrible. But it was a crime of passion. Murder/suicide—he did it because it was the only way they could be together."

"I feel sick."

"Why not let it be for a while. Get some rest."

She let him go that night, but the following weekend, they made love. Afterwards, he asked her to marry him. Anna recognized it for the gentle ultimatum that it was. She said yes. What she didn't say was that, with her eyes closed and Cam's hands on her, she'd been back in that tent with Mac. Like Belle, she could keep secrets.

She has always *loved* him; he's good and kind. She loves him now. They've been married five years and luck has been with them. Or at least she thought she was lucky, thought she'd finally grown up, grown into an ordinary life, marriage, a good job, summer canoe trips.

But they're on this camping trip because, in her words, they need, "time alone together." Punctuate it differently and you have another meaning. Time alone, together. Was it so surprising he'd reached out to someone else?

Everything about life in the city falls away when they're on the river. No phones, no urban noise or distractions. The pace of their forward motion is set by weather and the river itself, neither of which they can direct. Camping trips, she realizes, are basically a reprieve from the modern illusion of control. Here, nature is the arbiter, dispenser of storms and clear skies, and as they flow down these waterways, hauling the canoe over portages and beaver dams, crossing small lakes to find the outlet to another river or the same one, she feels their journey as a series of long and fluid paragraphs, punctuated by those moments when they see or hear something: a cluster of blue flags, tinier than their urban cousin the iris, living short but beautiful lives among upright grasses that almost obscure them from view; loons popping to the surface out of the depths, their elegant profiles sliding across the shining or brooding surface of the lake until they dive again; the barely discernible V behind the flat head of a swimming beaver; a family of otters playing an otter-ine game of hide-and-seek with their canoe; and that thing, whatever it was, sinuous as silk, that emerged from beneath a cedar root and slipped into the water. Mink, Cam said, but maybe marten. And the glimpse of something big and dark through the trees, twigs snapping as it retreats. It's when she's paddling, with Cam behind her, that she has most felt at ease in her life; the inner river of memories matched by the outer, she still marvels at how she could be both awash in the past and alert to the momentary gifts of the environment they're paddling through: edge-habitat, the *riparian* corridor, she loves the word, thinks it sounds like *repair*, which is what they're doing here.

They pull up at a portage sign, 530 metres. Before Cam lifts the canoe onto his shoulders, he places the backpack containing their clothes and sleeping bags on Anna's back.

When did she first suspect? At various times their schedules have been so busy that both could have managed an outside relationship. Perhaps she had been more aware of her own feelings. She carried a torch for Mac, still, but never did anything about it beyond feeling pleasure when he called every few months. She talked to Kay now, too, and felt particularly adult in overcoming her guilt, although, of course, they never talked about *that*.

No, Cam's "lapse"—is that, she hopes, all it is?—came as a complete surprise. Questioned, he said little more than it was a "woman at work," and, that it "happened" over a few months.

"Is it still going on?"

"No."

"Can you tell me why?"

"Why it's not going on?"

God no, she thought, with the sudden understanding that their marriage might not have been the incentive for the affair to stop. "Why it started."

"She's younger. That's not the reason," he quickly added, "but when we were together, it was just the two of us."

The night he read Belle's journal entry, he'd said, "I wouldn't mind if it was just about us, sometimes."

Just about us, she thinks as they come out of the portage after their second trip, this time carrying the food bag and tent. More smartweed. They load up the canoe and set out. Just about us: is it too late?

Last night, their first away from the city, she lay awake for a long while, mapping the scuttling of night creatures: toward, away, closer, too close! It was just the usual parade of "four-inch bears" as Cam refers to them, chipmunks and deer mice in their nocturnal search for food.

They see the orange tent sign at a distance and paddle to it. She climbs out of the bow and picks her way up the shoreline. Cam stays in the stern, his paddle out and wedged in a crevice between boulders. Over the years they've evolved this system; he won't begin to unload until she's done a quick tour and given her approval. After all it will be their bedroom and living room for the next fifteen hours. She walks past a grill leaning against the blackened rocks of the fire pit. On the ground of the clearing is a layer of pine needles, laced through with the long ropey roots of the trees that shed them. Someone has nailed a board between two pines to use as a shelf. There's a flat spot off to the left and two paths into the trees. One will lead to the thunder-box, the other, possibly, to an additional place for a tent. Maybe they'll pitch back there.

She's turning to walk back to the canoe when she hears the short exhalation of breath. She wheels around. There, fifty metres down the path where she hoped to pitch their tent, there's something large and dark. A bear. It—she? He?—is half in shadow, its hindquarters bathed in late sunlight. Anna's hand moves instinctively to her knife. The bear raises its big head, but it hasn't scented her, yet. Instead what breeze there is carries a rich rank odour to her.

Time slows. Can it see her? Clap your hands, a voice is screaming inside her head. Get to the canoe. But she does neither. Instead she takes a slow, liquid step toward the path, extricates the knife, her other hand reaching across to open the blade, slowly, smoothly, every action existing in a muffled cloak of deliberation, in air alternately shadowed and golden, viscous as a dream, each movement velvet and precise and yet dissolved in time, dissolving it.

Look Belle. The hair around the bear's shoulders bristles as it sniffs the air, the large head turning, small black eyes focusing on Anna. *I'll protect you, Belle.*

"Anna!"

She turns. Cam's head is jerking back and forth like a character in a cartoon. For a fraction of a second she has a wild urge to laugh, but then she sees the fear in his eyes. With one hand he raises his paddle in the air and swings it in a crazy arc. The other hand reaches out to grab her. A fine mist of spittle settles on her cheek as he yells, "For fuck's sake!"

His bruising grip on her arm hurts. She pulls her arm away and turns to look down the path. Nothing there now, just dust motes in a shaft of sunlight. Cam's paddle drops to the ground, he slumps to a seated position and puts his head in his hands. Anna, standing above him, reaches out and touches his hair, slick with sweat.

"I smelled it, Cam," she says that night in the tent. They've moved to the next site, halfway down the lake, and it is dusk by then. Cam had put up the tent while she cooked a simple meal. He hadn't spoken to her once or even looked at her, busying himself, instead, with the dozen tiny tasks of setting camp. "I smelled that odour on him."

"What are you talking about?"

"About Paul, after he came back to the tent." She is crying now, in gulping sobs, "I know it's crazy."

He is on his back, staring up at the nylon roof of the tent.

"It was like I was in her story, or in her head, the wild smell on him …"

"The bear?"

"Yes, no! Paul, I mean—he smelled like the bear."

"Anna. Enough."

"Wait! I understand it now. If you hadn't been behind me I'd have walked right up to the bear. It's in here, "she pressed her hand to her chest," in all of us and sometimes it goes off, like a shot or something, or, I dunno, it's something you can't control. It's why she was attracted to him, and, maybe, it's why he killed her. I mean, he couldn't handle the wild part of himself, you know," she trails off. She can see by his face he doesn't get it, and doesn't want to try.

Does it matter? Isn't this just her way of saying what he already knows? It was why he strapped on a parachute so soon after Trevor's death. It was why he could love her when she wasn't entirely capable of the same. There were no words you could wrap around it, though she has, just now, tried, though she has been trying for thirteen years to find a measurable reason or answer and then simply slipped through that invisible membrane as she walked toward the bear. She shivers—how close you can come, how exhilarating and seductive and potent it can be, keeping you moving toward the thing you shouldn't. The wild and unknown, the pre-known.

"Time for sleep, Anna." He sounds spent.

She dozes, wakes, and lies for what seems an hour with a full bladder, finally leaving the tent and padding in bare feet to a tree, where she squats to relieve herself. After peeing, she stares at the astonishing profusion of stars, and in the blurry scarf of the Milky Way, her eyes focus on a moving prick of light, a satellite, orbiting the earth.

Except for a slight breeze soughing through the pine boughs, the woods are quiet. And there is a peace to it; for the first time in years she can feel her spirit moving beyond the confines of adamant memory. All those years ago, Belle said it: we earn our rest. Whether Cam can still love her remains to be seen; for now, it is her turn to give what he has earned, deep affection untainted by ghosts. Goodbye lovely, willful, imperfect sister.

Woman in Ice

In the weeks after Jan left he stripped the bedroom of her touch, folded up the burgundy bedspread, took down the burgundy and gold curtains and their irritating tasseled swags, packed up the decorative pillows—round, square, buttoned, and flapped, and one that he thought of as suitable only for a pygmy. These filled two garbage bags. So that he could read in bed, he kept three ordinary bed pillows. He took down the wall sconces and snugged candles into two shoe boxes; he wrapped several square glass candle holders in the burgundy shawl that, in his recollection, Jan had never worn though she'd often adjusted its position over the back of the chair. He put the lumpy package in a cardboard box along with some paperback mysteries and *Gourmet* magazines. He ousted the iron doorstopper in the shape of a hare. Then he stood for a few minutes staring at the floor in the corner, at a wide, round papier-mâché plate that held painted wooden balls of unknown purpose, giving them one last dispassionate glance before he dumped them into a garbage bag that he planned to stuff into the maw of the charity dumpster. He moved the decor-matching Kleenex box into the bathroom for when he ran out of TP and allowed the coaster, if not the bedside table, to become marked with coffee circles which were routinely diluted by condensation drips from the beer or glass of scotch he brought to bed at the other end of the day. He unpacked the old Hudson's Bay blanket and two quilts his grandmother had made, and for really cold nights he could zip open his down sleeping bag as a comforter, because from now on he'd sleep with the furnace off and the window cracked open an inch, and he didn't bother replacing the curtains because every once in a while a man needed his sky straight up, even though the light pollution of the city drowned out all but a handful of tossed and sparkling stars. Now, with his clothes over the chair in the corner and framed photos—once banished—of his parents and the farm on the dresser, the walls of this room could be the screen for a handful of bittersweet memories. To aid in these, he'd blown up and framed a snapshot of a smiling young woman who stood in a snowy landscape among stunted black spruce. Unruly curls escaped her toque, spilling over the wolverine collar of a puffy red parka. She was wearing the white moon boots favoured by regulars in the North.

He had "come home" from the northern reaches of the province knowing his job in seismic was over. So was his marriage. And something else, a loss even more devastating: any possibility of true happiness. Jan was slow to pick up on the rift—it took her two-thirds of a year and the redecoration of both the living and dining rooms—but quick to seize on the injustice. Her anger made sense. That he had laid low until she noticed was an unforgivable lapse of respect and responsibility in a marriage that, if you included its final arid months, had lasted a decade. But he was wholly and completely occupied in something that took all his energy, mourning the loss, not of his marriage but another much deeper love, without revealing it on the surface. He found work immediately in a local engineering firm, working long hours out of choice. When, in the first few months of his return, his wife accused him of male frigidity, he wanted to shake her because it was true. He was figuratively, if no longer literally, cold all the time now. Making love, even for old time's sake and with the woman who was legally still his wife, was too much a betrayal of a ghost.

Jan had previously possessed a brittle sort of anger, but for a short time that summer she was a powder keg; as the temperature hovered in the eighties, she threw dishes and tantrums. When neither of these worked—he didn't care about china patterns; he tuned out the yelling and slamming of doors—she sought and found her ultimate distraction: she decided to throw a party. He suspected that she couldn't bear to waste her year of decorating. They had always differed in their approaches to entertaining. He liked beer and pizza or chili after an afternoon of shinny or Frisbee with friends. The lavish dinner was her focus during their last months of cohabitation. On the scheduled day, Darrel walked though the house wondering how much it had all cost. There were expensive-looking floral arrangements in the front hall and on the sideboard and coffee table. There were new towels and flowers in both bathrooms. A six-course catered menu for eighteen was probably close to a thousand dollars and that was before the liquor, wine, and the designer outfit laid out on the bed in the master bedroom, where Darrel no longer slept. He had no idea who would be coming through the door at dusk; Jan hadn't consulted with him about the guest list. She had become adept at the combined mingling and networking that her position in the community demanded. She managed a branch of the RBC and sat on a variety of boards. He was resigned to enduring the party in the hopes of maintaining some degree of amicability as they parted for good.

When the evening arrived, he was a competent host, taking coats, offering drinks and refills, talking with everyone about the weather or sports or local politics. As the dinner began, he toasted his wife for the "beautiful improvements to this house." He could not bear to say home. The clinking of cutlery and the creaking of chairs under their well-heeled guests was a swan song to an era that for him had never really begun. He wouldn't miss that future for a second, but he could acknowledge a certain artistry in Jan's planning of a peculiarly middle-class confection, a lovely surface with nothing inside.

He stood as the dinner plates were being cleared; he needed a smoke. In recent months, he had returned to this college habit, keeping a pack going, sometimes not smoking for days on end, occasionally walking by the river so that he could look out over the water and have two or three in a row, lighting one from the butt of the other. He passed through the kitchen and nodded quickly to the catering staff. There were two men and two women, all young and attractive; the demeanor of the younger man was precise, a little feminine. They looked like college students or young wannabe artists and actors. They scraped and piled dirty dishes and readied trays to take out to the dining room. The large rented coffee urn was beginning to emit its odour of decaf French roast. He opened the sliding doors. As he stepped through, one of the women said, "Careful of the ice sculpture."

Ah yes, he thought, Jan's "surprise" dessert, which she had referred to a half-dozen times and which interested him as much as a trip to the dentist, except that now, viewing the foil-shrouded trolley next to the barbeque, he wondered what its inclusion added to the evening's tally. It was a chilly October night, cold enough outside to keep the ice from melting. He didn't bother to take a peek, and after a couple of long drags, he knelt and pushed his half-smoked cigarette into the moist, cold earth of the closest flowerbed. Passing through the kitchen and out the other end, he slipped into the hall washroom, washed his hands, and gargled some mouthwash. He looked at himself in the mirror.

"You've got flecks of amber in your eyes," she had said. Oh, Kathryn. A wave of sorrow hit him. He lowered the toilet seat cover and sat for a minute with his head in his hands.

Jan was standing beside his chair when he returned to the dining room. As he slipped into his seat, she whispered a terse, "We couldn't wait." The two male waiters stood at the other end of the table. They pushed the sculpture on its platter halfway down the cleared centre surface and went back into the kitchen.

Everyone was saying: "Oh my" and "Well done." There was even a little round of applause.

The woman to his left, a colleague of Jan's, was nattering about real estate values in the neighbourhood. He pretended to listen, but his thoughts were far away. The dessert was being served with a certain amount of theatricality: individual fig puddings set aflame. From the head of the table, Darrel examined his end of the sculpture. He had a foreshortened view. It seemed to be an animal, something sleek and curved like a seal.

Talking and clinking and various sounds of pleasure flowed around the table. Jan rose and announced a move to the living room for coffee and liqueurs. Before leaving the dining room Darrel looked back over his shoulder.

He might have doused the candles on the sideboard or checked to make sure no-one had left a purse dangling from the arm of a chair, any of a half-dozen small gestures of manly propriety that seemed required by the tenor of the evening, and which he felt he owed his wife after his minor nicotine treason. But he did none of these things. He did nothing because for the first time, he saw the whole of the centrepiece. The ice—previously otter-like and just beginning to melt—revealed its real shape, that of a kneeling and tucked woman. The world momentarily stilled on its axis. When his breath came again it was with a gasp. Something else was rising—the acid and the sweet, bile and undigested desert. He blundered through the kitchen and into the backyard, retracing earlier steps. Hanging over the same flowerbed where a half hour earlier he had put out his half-smoked cigarette, he vomited.

The young waiter stood in the doorway: "Are you okay?"

He made a dry growling sound. His throat burned, and he flinched from the taste of vomit. He swallowed and blinked.

"I'm fine," he said, and then, as an afterthought, "It's not the food." Darrel shook his head to clear it.

"I need a favour," he said before describing his key ring on the hall table. "And don't worry, I've only had a beer and a glass of wine."

When the young guy came out again with the keys, he wouldn't take any money. Darrel allowed himself a small smile. It was simply understood sometimes, that a man had to get the hell out of Dodge.

Darrel walked around the side of the house and out across his lawn. As he got into his truck, he looked back. The windows of his house shone gold. It looked, he thought, like a happy home. Inside, on the dining room table, was a weeping icy centrepiece cast from a mold. The mold mimicked a famous Rodin sculpture of a young woman slumped in grief against a rock—frozen, melting, soon to disappear.

So Jan knew. That's what ten years of marriage gave you, a kind of sub-knowledge that was at its most creative when it was also at its most cruel.

MEROMIXIS

This morning it was Tom's plan to fish Emerald Lake; the challenge appealed, plus it came with the guarantee of solitude. Nobody else seemed to bother with a lake that wouldn't yield more than half a dozen fish in an entire season. The lake was meromictic; steep surrounding banks prevented wind from getting at its surface and stymied the process by which most lakes took oxygen-rich water into their depths. It was oxygen deprivation that had given the lake its unearthly hue and created a dearth of the usual muck and tumble. So, none of the usual arrowhead and pickerel weed, lilies with their wide circular pads and egg-cup flowers, where ducks, herons, fish, frogs, turtles, crayfish, and otters might weave in and out of each other's domains, the sometimes peaceable, sometimes predatory warp and weft of species. And so, to match that strange pale colour, there was a special sort of quietness because of all the creatures that didn't come to call.

He knew the time every year when the ice was likely to break up, and the best months for this or that fish. There was something fine about being out on the water just as the sun was clearing the tips of the white pines. Coffee never tasted as good as out of the plastic cup of the thermos, its aroma mixed with the smell of gasoline and the fishy stink of his tackle box. The wiry hair of his collie under his fingertips, a line in the water waiting for that first impetuous tug, it was more than worth getting up for, it was the kind of thing to measure a life by, the even-handed open-endedness of a man, a fishing rod, and a small cedar boat.

Ordinarily he'd have brought the dog. She was well-behaved in the boat, sniffing with curiosity at the fish he took off his hook, standing guard as they twitched and flopped. But she'd injured her paw two days earlier, and he didn't want to take a chance on the wound going septic.

Later he'd understand that her absence was a stroke of luck.

He was using an old cedar strip—his grandfather's—with a flat stern that accommodated a little motor. The one-horse looked like an egg-beater, but she trolled just fine and hardly added weight to the boat if he needed to portage.

Tom fished, very occasionally, with others—his next-door neighbour Milton, one or two fellows from work. He went along with them because they asked, but since his father's death he felt that fishing, for the most part, was best done alone. This too, he would realize later, was an ingredient in the long list that allowed for the miracle.

He drove for about forty minutes, slowly, enjoying the moist air through his half-opened window. He liked the feeling of being the only one in the world, watching the treetops take shape against a gradually paling sky, the first licks of gold squinting through a fretwork of branches. He kept the radio off. At a spot without evident markings he pulled over onto the shoulder and parked the truck. Here, a steep gravelly slope fell away from the county road, allowing access by foot to a shallow sandy cove. In short order, the canoe was off the top of the truck and on his shoulders. Descending through slanted shadows to the beach, he placed each foot carefully. A pebble shifted, then several; he slid a little.

"Steady now," he said. The sound of his words momentarily stilled the singing sparrow, the drumming of the black-backed woodpecker.

"Hey," he said, addressing the birds and trees to either side of his path, "it's only me."

At the water's edge he bent his head, allowing the bow to rest on the sand. In one fluid movement, he backed out from underneath the yoke and flipped the canoe off to his right. He took his shoes off, rolled his pant legs up and waded into the turquoise-green water, pulling the canoe until it floated free. Puffs of fine silt rose where his feet disturbed the soft lake bottom. He got in, arranged his gear, and paddled until the water was deep enough to drop the motor.

A loon called, defining the perimeter of the lake with a haunting boomerang of sound. Straight ahead, two birds swam in circles, carving lines on glass, backlit by the new day. The closer of the two dipped its beak and disappeared. In his imagination he followed, piercing the veil between air and water, diving, diving.

Emerald Lake had a character, defined in part by the thwarted interaction of the sky and wind above with the depth and stillness below. Air and water: two elements that didn't reflect so much as leave each other alone, an aerial climate affecting the aquatic world it couldn't touch. Like men and women, Tom thought.

He flipped a switch and pulled the starter cord, and the little motor flared to life. The bow lifted as he took the canoe into an arc. The fishing here was poor but he always came back, seduced by that astonishing colour. In a small velvet box on his dresser was a pair of emerald earrings that had been his mother's. Set in gold, the two faceted ovals were like drops of the lake, distilled. Before she died, she'd given them to him—for his wife, the one he didn't have yet. It wasn't that certain women hadn't attracted his interest. But then they had eluded him, leaving town for Sudbury or Toronto to pursue careers or romances. They returned to Chapleau to visit in sleek cars or new vans driven by men whose jackets of creamy leather or bright nylon didn't show a trace of fish guts or motor oil.

He flipped open his tackle box and chose a fat neon lure. The sun was above the trees but not yet hitting the water; he'd switch to a dark lure when it did. Pity, he thought, that women weren't like fish, that you couldn't just put out your line and wait for the tug.

In the past weeks, he'd noticed the blond at the gas station; why was someone so attractive filling tanks in this neck of the woods? The baggy overalls didn't disguise a great body; he tried not to stare. That smile. Tom never could think of a thing to say beyond "Beautiful day, eh?" or "We've got a bit of cloud," like some dopey weatherman telling her what she could already see. He'd drive off with a certain fatalism; she'd be gone in the fall like all the others.

The sun was coming across the water toward him now. He poured another coffee from the thermos and unwrapped his second sandwich, eating one half and balancing the other on the thwart. He switched lures and cast again then started to troll, one hand on the tiller, the other holding the rod. After a few moments he clamped it into the holder at the side of the canoe and finished the sandwich and coffee then rinsed the cup over the side.

The lake was shaped something like a peanut with two relatively distinct bays. He swung the canoe alongside the peninsula that separated them. As he drew clear of the channel he felt the hit and for the next ten minutes he was aware of nothing else, alternately locking and reeling in line. Then it went slack. When he hauled the last few feet of it out of the water, the hook and lure were gone.

"Damn," he said. But the fight confirmed the presence of fish beneath his boat.

He tied on an Aglia Long and made a couple of casts. As the line stretched out he saw a flash off the right side of his bow as something—a record breaker—broke the surface. Could a fish that large be in Emerald Lake?

Could it be an otter? The corona of spray was just now subsiding, wide ripples emanating out from the centre.

There! Another leap of silver. He was staring so hard at the spot where it had emerged that for a long moment he didn't register the shadow approaching underwater, but his refocusing was automatic. His mouth dropped open. He yanked the tiller hard, and as the canoe came around the thing slowed, stopped, and floated just beneath the surface.

He could hear his heart. It was no longer possible to ignore the various components, the tail, the hair drifting across a face, the pale arms …

"You don't exist." His voice was tight.

What broke the surface was a hand curled in a loose fist, drawn back, and then flicked forward, fingers opening in release. The object arced neatly and landed with a plop in the boat. He bent to retrieve it. A length of fishing line protruded from something serpentine and dark: his lure was snagged on a thick lock of hair.

His hand flew to the back of his own head in empathy.

"Shit!" he said "I'm so sorry…"

But she was gone.

How could the brain do that—reject information and yet catalogue it at the same time? What *had* he seen through the rippling surface of the water? Full breasts. Drifting dark hair had mostly obscured her face. From the waist down she was plump and shimmering, and though that part of her was the length and contour of legs, it was not like legs at all. Her head and shoulders had never broken the surface of the water. She'd just *hung there,* her torso and shoulders suspended, tail fin in constant motion.

It was hard to describe her in those words—fin, scales, tail. His mind skittered around the piscine references.

He didn't sleep at all that night, not even after he stroked himself to release, picturing those breasts, the momentary glimpse he'd had of dark eyes. Sunday found him motionless in the old swing chair on the veranda, the dog beside him with her head in his lap.

He shook himself out of lethargy by mid-afternoon, painted the shed door and turned over sections of his vegetable patch. The activity was good, but what he really wanted was to get back in his truck and drive to the lake, strip off his clothes and dive, dive until he found—what? A hallucination? A dream?

Instead he went to work the following morning. It was the height of summer, and he drove past the little unmarked turn-off almost daily, en route to Borden Lake and Mulligan Bay. Each time Tom felt the tug, a cellular connection to the cove so strong he wanted to stop the truck and run down to the water. What if he didn't see her again?

What if he did?

Tom was distracted now, all the time. At night he often fell asleep in his veranda chair. He dreamt that Emerald Lake was being drained and as the water level lowered, more and more people appeared along its shore. They stood staring into the water, pointing and laughing. A group of children began to throw stones. He woke himself shouting, "Stop!" Tess padded into the room. She squatted at his feet and looked up at him, cocking her head.

"I have to see her," he said to the dog. The clock on the mantle showed 2:00 a.m.

He walked through the kitchen to the side door, Tess trotting behind him.

"No girl," he said quietly.

Her response was a low growl. "Oh shit," he said, "okay, but you're staying in the truck."

He drove quickly. At the unmarked spot on Highway 101, he pulled the truck off the side of the road.

"Stay," he said firmly, holding Tess back with one hand as he got out.

He kicked off his sandals and stripped off his t-shirt, shorts, and boxers. The doubt of the last few days was gone; if she was in the lake, she'd know he was in it. The moon was high in the sky.

He waded in. When the water reached his thighs he leaned forward. As his feet rose off the velvety sand, he heard a distant splash. He swam for ten minutes, occasionally raising his head to take his bearings. Slowing, he let his legs drop.

Her fingers at his elbows were a surprise. He felt something graze the inside of his ankles then rise along both calves, the tiny pick of scales rubbing against the inside of his knees and tugging gently at the hair on his thighs. The feeling was exquisite. He was getting an erection. She was buoying him up to the point that his chest was clear of the water but then her hands let go of his elbows and he sank. Treading water again, his right foot glanced off something soft and yielding. Her hands pried his thighs far apart. Heat flared through his groin. What was she doing? The body between his legs twisted.

She was *carrying* him. Repeated flicks of her torso and tail propelled them faster even than the cedar strip with its trolling motor. They slowed only as they neared the far shore of the lake. There were a couple of dead trees here, one of them half submerged, the base of it still on land. He took hold of a branch and raised his right leg as she executed a neat tuck beneath him.

Then, nothing.

Had she abandoned him so soon? The exhilaration of the ride was gone; he could feel the almost painful draining of adrenalin from his limbs. He turned his head toward the shore, scrutinized the thick mass of trees. The idea of bushwhacking back to his truck was overwhelming; it would take hours. He felt rather than heard a shift in the pressure of the water and turned to face the lake.

There—again the strange stasis, part float, part levitation, just out of reach, so that he had to take in the whole, compelling, unbelievable combination. He made a beckoning gesture above the surface—think this through, he was saying to himself, she's underwater—and so he dropped to his knee. Submerged, he tried again. She responded, effortlessly closing the short distance, her outstretched hand reaching for his, pulling him away from the shallows into deeper water, the other arm coming in a slow arabesque and then just a finger touching his ear, sliding up along his hairline and across his brow, tracing a delicate curve that circled his nostril, his lips—he was living by touch now, recognizing her as she recognized him, her finger descending in a single sure line from Adam's apple to his navel. Then her fingers spread and descended toward his groin while her other hand played in his fingers, lacing in and out, pushing gently, tip to tip, followed by feathery touches on his palm.

No air left. Tom pointed up, patting his chest. She turned him around with her two hands, forcefully, and raised them both to the surface. He sucked in air with a gasp. She pushed him back toward the log then pressed herself into his back, her nose burrowing into his wet hair, breasts against his skin. Now she was turning him, sliding herself onto his chest, leaning into him against the log, and they were kissing. He reached down and cupped her breasts.

He directed her hands to the branches on the log. "Hold on," he said and he slid his hands down her arms and bent over her, kissing her breasts, first one then the other. Her skin, sweet and firm, tasted of lake, of summer. He splayed his fingers and explored the skin of her tummy where it turned to scale. It felt odd but wonderful. His hand, now underwater, glided over her freely, from one hip to another and down. He was looking for an opening. He wrapped his legs around her and his lips, hungry, found hers. She reached down with a hand and stroked him and then in one deft move she'd slipped out from underneath him.

Again!

A fluttering tickle on his stomach: her hair. He felt her mouth wrap around his penis. He groaned. Reaching down, he expected to touch her head or shoulders, but his hand met scales. He slid his palm up under the ends of hair and almost laughed.

It wasn't on the front at all.

Small waves flapped against the log. He stared unseeing at a sky littered with stars. When the orgasm took him, he let out a small high whoop. As his penis slithered free the pressure against his legs became a solid shove.

For a terrifying moment he wondered if she meant to drown him. Crablike, he scrambled backwards in the fine silt and over slick logs along the bottom. She'd swum away, but he could hear her coming back, flicking her tail from side to side, flip-flop, flip-flop, water like loops of moonlit pearls bouncing off her tail. She pulled at the hand he put forward to touch her. He was swimming alongside and then above her as she slipped in under him, and this time his body cooperated, legs circling her waist as they cut through the channel at delicious speed.

Just shy of the beach she dove. Her tail caught his shoulders a glancing blow, and he was thrust forward, water up his nose and in his eyes. Coughing, he floundered up the slope of the beach. He turned in time to see a series of circles emanating from a point some metres distant.

"Bye," he called, plaintive as a loon.

From behind and up the slope Tom heard barking. He pulled on his clothes and sandals then walked up the steep path to his truck. As he got in behind the wheel, Tess gave his face a lick. "Quit it, I'm wet enough already." She raised herself on her two front legs and began to sniff delicately along his leg towards his crotch, then the far leg and his chest.

"Goddamn canine FBI."

The next day he didn't wake till eleven. He puttered around the house until late afternoon. When he remembered he had no potatoes for dinner, he hopped in the truck and headed to the IGA. On the way home he stopped for gas. The pretty young woman was filling another car. After it departed she stayed at the gas bar, leaning nonchalantly against the pump.

One look at the blond curls escaping from beneath her bandana and one long leg swinging across and over the other, and he realized that the events of last night had set a new and impossible standard. The template in his mind consisted of dark floating hair, round pale breasts—and an iridescent tail.

He handed the young blond his credit card. When she came back with the plastic tray he signed his receipt without making eye contact. He was enough of a gentleman, though, to tip his cap before he drove off.

Back in his kitchen, Tom cooked potatoes, green beans, and a pork chop. He prepared a plate but ate standing, turning and leaning against the counter. At dusk he headed out the door. So began a long sojourn of evenings at the lake: straight home from work, a quick nap and a simple meal before Emerald Lake. Tess no longer insisted on joining him in the truck. Instead she sat in the doorway to the living room and cocked her head. "Again?" she seemed to be saying.

His lover. He allowed himself to think of her that way. What was harder was all the rest. His lover had a tail, scales, lived in a lake; his lover was a *mermaid*.

They had exchanged no words, but she was keeping her head out of the water for longer and longer periods after they made love. Sensing her desire to listen—but unsure if she understood—he began to talk about himself and his childhood, fishing with his father, collecting berries with his mom. Soon he was leaving work earlier to have more time with her, and though he managed to fulfil his warden duties, he understood he was walking a fine line between "selective" efficiency and negligence.

At home there were storm windows to install and a cord of wood to split before winter, but the screens stayed on, and one afternoon, chopping wood, he simply reduced every log on the block to kindling. Whenever he wasn't at the lake he was devising and rejecting possible solutions. A tank would attract questions and ultimately be too small. A pond could be dug on his property with a back-hoe and dump truck, machinery he could borrow from the ministry. But he doubted he could make one deep enough to avoid problems with coyotes, bears, and even wolves. And how would he move her?

One evening in early October, Tom entered the lake and swam out to their usual meeting spot. The water had grown noticeably colder, and he was glad not only for the insulation but the buoyancy of his new full-length wet suit and flippers. Five minutes passed, then ten, before he felt the tell-tale push of water in front of him and the light flick of her fingers between his knees. When they arrived at the shore he tried to postpone sex in order to tell her, in whatever way he could—he still wasn't sure she understood anything he said—that he couldn't wait that long in the water, not in these temperatures. But she was hungrier for his touch than ever, yanking at the zipper of the rubber suit. There was a look in her eyes, both determined and forlorn. The changing colour of the trees and the nip in the air was impossible to ignore.

It occurred to him that there was a season to their "mating." Was it coming to an end?

After, he pulled her toward him in the shallows. The look she gave him reminded him, fleetingly, of Tess, sad and a little reproachful. She made as if to pull him back into the water.

"Not yet," he said. In rapid succession he listed the solutions he'd already dismissed: the tank, the backyard pond.

"I even thought of building something out over the water, right here," he said. The look of alarm on her face told him to stop. "Not to trap you," he added quickly. "Just so we can be together …"

Her head was turned toward the far shore, away from him. Tom began to speak quickly.

"Maybe I could set it back in the trees, put in a stove. And then, once it freezes I can either ski across or hike in through the woods. I won't be able to stay with you in the water." His words were gushing out,"But I'll keep a hole open in the ice. We can …"

Talk? She never had. Visit? Have tea?

The moon was out. It shone on the water around her, on her glistening hair and white shoulders. She pulled at his arm, and he let her tow him toward deeper water where he straddled her for the ride back. At the cove, she pushed him off and then surfaced beside him, turning him toward her. For a long moment they stared into each other's eyes. He sensed the finality in it. She pressed her lips to his and then, with a final splash of that powerful tail, she was gone.

Tom drove out the next night and the next and swam to their spot. She didn't come. The following night he brought the canoe and paddled a circuit of the entire lake. No sign. He kept at it for another week, returning each night from his vigil to fall into an exhausted sleep. She appeared in his dreams, swimming away from him, growing smaller.

He turned back to his work with the concentration he had reserved for her, taking on extra shifts, anything to distract himself. There was a melancholy reassurance in travelling the lakes and rivers it was his responsibility to check.

The night of the first snowfall, he got in his truck and drove, helplessly, out to the lake. But at the spot where he had so often pulled off to park, he stopped. His hands gripped the steering wheel, his eyes closed for a moment and then, filling his lungs with the still-cold air in the cab of his truck, he executed a decisive U-turn, tires slipping on snow, and drove back in the direction he'd come. At his own driveway he only hesitated for a second, continuing past his mailbox and into town.

The local tavern was quiet, just a few regulars. He sat at a corner table. A door behind the bar opened and a woman emerged from a back room. It was the leggy blond from the gas station. When she reached his table she smiled.

"You don't usually come in," she said.

"No," he said.

There was a longish pause.

"Beer?"

He shook his head. "Scotch, neat."

When she returned with the drink he started to dig in his pocket.

"You can run a tab."

"I probably won't stay." He extricated his wallet and pulled out a ten.

"I could've sworn you would."

"Pardon?"

"You look like you need to drown your sorrows," she said, the corners of her mouth lifting in sympathy.

He let out a weary laugh. "It's that obvious?"

"You want some company?"

He meant to resist. He meant to leave after downing his drink, but instead he ordered another and pulled out a chair as she came to deliver it, and when she sat down they exchanged names.

"You're not from around here, Carrie."

"My brother moved here a few years ago. I was at loose ends for the summer, and he offered free room and board. I got the job at the gas station through a friend of his. Anyway, my university courses don't start till January. It was getting too cold to stand around pumping gas, so now," she mimicked the action of lowering the handle on a beer tap, "I'm pumping beer."

She'd be leaving town soon. The desire to unburden rose in his throat. Finally, he could tell someone the truth or at least half of it: he'd fallen in love with a beautiful woman. Carrie had brought him a glass of water with his second whiskey. He picked up the glass, swirled its contents.

"She kind of moved in a different world," he said.

"Summer love," said Carrie, "with someone from away. It happens."

He smiled to himself: away. Yes, very.

"She wasn't much of a communicator."

"You don't know why she ended it?"

"I think she felt we were," he paused and then, as if he were only now acknowledging it, "incompatible."

"These days, we assume men are avoiding commitment," Carrie said. "But women can be, too."

"She was from a different ... environment, I guess you could say" Tom sighed. "I guess she needed to return to it."

"Or," Carrie had an amused expression on her face, "she stopped seeing you because it worked."

"What do you mean?"

"She got what she wanted."

"Which was ...?"

"The best genetic material in town."

He just stared at her.

"I'd say we're talking biological clock."

A group of latecomers came through the door and she rose. "You don't have to take my advice, but in a situation like this you can mope or," she flashed him a sympathetic grin, "you can say to yourself, she picked *me*."

Tom left a generous tip on his table and gave her a quick salute on the way out. Even before he was out of his truck he was counting on his fingers. He had to do it three times before he got it right. Conception might have happened as early as July.

Every morning from then on, he took the little canoe out and paddled to their cove; he didn't allow himself to expect anything, and she didn't show herself. The days were getting shorter and chillier. Before long he was moving through the gelatinous beginnings of ice; flat pans of it clicked against the hull. In December, a cold snap sealed the lake's surface. After two weeks of below-zero temps—enough to ensure the ice would hold his weight—he returned, sliding through thick drifts to get to the lake edge. His path across it intersected with the diagonal tracks of marten and deer. One perfect imprint of hawk wings around a small section of disturbed snow indicated the last seconds of life for a racing chipmunk or squirrel. He walked until he reached the spot where, for two and a half months, he'd waited in anticipation of her touch.

He'd brought a small shovel. Now he pushed it ahead of him, turning and turning until he'd cleared an oval twice his length and width. The ice was thick and clear, a little milky along the cracks where one segment had shifted against another. The shovel was set aside.

Tom stretched out on his back first. The sky was pale pewter. He turned his head toward the shore, to the black trees. Now he rolled onto his stomach and raised himself on his elbows. With his mitts he polished the surface below his head and shoulders. He stared down through liquid made solid, the soft made hard. Sealed off, the unearthly green of Emerald Lake was darker, brooding. Somewhere on this lake she was keeping a hole open for herself and the tiny body she nurtured inside, and he respected her animal need to do this alone, as silent and self-contained as he had always been. He was cold but he didn't mind. He would return every day up to and after spring break-up, up to and after the months he had counted, excitedly, on his fingers. Until he knew. *Either way,* he would keep coming. The lake was kin to him now.

DOWNHILL

She is a long woman. For years now, she has been stretched out on a bed—though kinked might be the better word—a landscape eroding, her body colonized by multiple sclerosis. The disease has its own vocabulary and associated activities: atrophy, extension, contraction, physiotherapy, hydrotherapy. It has been ages since they worried about occupational therapy. She is no longer a homemaker; the years of pulling her lower limbs off the bed or couch and leaning on furniture to drag herself around the apartment are over. Gone are the sandwiches and simple dinners. They had to be simple, in those days she thought her way through everything beforehand to conserve her strength. She thought her way through sex too, planning which moves she could make, could afford to, to have enough left at the end to shimmy her nightgown down over her hips and pat him on the back or squeeze his hand so that he'd know she still enjoyed it, still wanted to, even though her body seemed so unresponsive. Now she has caretakers of her own: cheerful and opinionated aides, nurses dispensing pills in paper cups, and orderlies who speak no English but sometimes whistle, which is a diversion. Three times a week therapists work to bend her unyielding long legs or squeeze another tube of foam into each rigidly folded fist. They're good girls, kind and smart, and they know they can't do a thing for her, and she knows it too, but they don't pity her, and that's something.

Most infrequently, the chief caretaker, Dr. Sutton—Audrey knows his first name is Stan because she's heard the nurses talking about him—drops in for a visit, at least that's what he calls it. He rarely stays for more than a minute or two. Before he leaves, he often prescribes another drug: "Something new and useless with an unpronounceable name," says her son. And every Friday, a hairdresser named Leona comes to give them all the same starched-and-soon-flattened bouffant.

"How are we today, dear?"

How should they answer the ubiquitous and rhetorical question? "Dying dear, thanks," or "Catheterized but proud! And you?"

MS has not deprived Audrey of a sense of humour. She has secretly dubbed the hairdresser "the female impersonator," because though Leona is, of course, a woman, every item of her femininity is amplified and over-produced: fake nails, garish lips, obvious pancake make-up, and a ludicrously piled beehive. Leona bustles under it as if under an independent helmet, colouring it according to the season. She favours blue-black for winter and the palest champagne for spring. When, one autumn day, she strolls in under a corona of flaming red, Audrey pipes up, "Leona, you blend in with the leaves!"

The hairdresser's hands always smell of nicotine as she barges from bed to bed with her little trolley of plastic curlers, nets, and spray, working on the women one at a time but holding forth to the room in general, certain of the efficacy of a love life, second-hand.

"I met Phil at a ballroom dancing class. Can that man move," Leona swivels her broad hips in tan stretch pants, rubber-soled shoes squeaking on linoleum. And later, in a not so *sotto voce* aside to one of the orderlies, "Poor dears, they're not getting it any more, do 'em good to hear about a little fun." As if we were bed-wetting children in a nursery, Audrey thinks, instead of bed-wetting adults dying slowly on a ward in the Riverdale Hospital.

Still, it's a break in the endlessness of days in that toothpaste-green room, and so when Leona's ample bust enters the room, "forty-four double Ds and proud of it!" Audrey pulls a smile from her limited kit bag of expressions and chimes in with the general chorus of "fine" and waits for the predictable scrape of thirty-four plastic picks on a tender scalp.

Audrey hates her weekly hairdo, but it's an improvement over the alternative: limp strands at the front and a tatty mass at the back because all day long her head rubs at the starched pillowcase, first toward the window, then toward the door. She likes to see who's coming. She likes to know whether it's raining outside or clear. Little things matter, keeping track of storms or the humidex, comparing her own observations with reports made at the end of the evening news by the weatherman behind the big Plexiglas map of Ontario. He wields thick markers in both hands as he talks, each hand scribbling numbers and symbols over hundreds of square miles: round suns and puffy clouds, snowflakes fat as Sudbury, raindrops slanting into the lake, accumulation in inches, daily highs and lows. She has no need of weather herself, rarely going out in it and only then from the hospital entrance to her son's van, from the van to her daughter's house or into her daughter's backyard when the sun is shining. But her son is a postie, and so she memorizes ambidextrous predictions; she marvels at the certainty with which the weatherman knows what he cannot know.

"Pissing rain today," John says, coming into the room on one of his visits, bending over his mother's bed and shaking his head like a dog to spray tiny droplets over her bedding. Or, "colder than a witch's tit." And sometimes his mini reports aren't spoken but mimed; even before he's kissed her, he might jump into a chair and, for the benefit of the entire room, bend in a racing crouch, pushing off with imaginary poles, or skate around the foot of her bed, feet sliding on the polished floor.

"Snow?" the ladies guess. "Freezing rain?"

"Two points to you, Mrs. Wilson," he says to the sour woman whose bed is across from Audrey's. "You're today's winner of The Great Canadian Weather Roulette." He brings them what they no longer have: a stiff breeze, a handful of snow, all things youthful and immediate.

She has so much more than some of the other women here. Even if Ted, her husband, rarely visits and her eldest son is on the other side of the world, she sees Donna and Teddie, and every other day the thing that keeps her fear inside, tamped down and in control. Because every other day, there's John.

Soon after she was hospitalized, John bought a van, an ex-ambulance, to transport her to Donna's place in Oakville for birthday parties and Sunday barbeques. For these outings, the nurses' aides spruce her up, dabbing on lipstick and shoe-horning her opened paperclip of a body into a lace-collared blouse and long skirt. Ted always manages to have a business meeting and Bob, her eldest, is in Nepal or India or Australia, searching for enlightenment that will not come and cannot change a thing.

Donna's doctor husband places newspapers and kerosene beneath the single apple tree in his backyard and contemplates the inventive cottony shapes that tent caterpillars have spun between branches.

He starts the barbeque then takes orders for drinks. He offers John a beer.

"Audrey," Doug clears his throat, "would you like a pop? Coke? Ginger ale?" His eyes are focussed just beyond her right ear.

"Ginger ale," she whispers, "would be fine," wishing the words were louder, wishing her voice didn't come out in a breathless squawk.

"Fine," he says, rubbing his palms together.

He goes back inside and brings out a tray of drinks. Donna has been in and out already, carrying bowls of potato salad and paper plates, dishes of sliced tomatoes and pickles. Teddie raises his arms to her, wanting to be carried.

"Doug," says Donna. "The highchair?"

Her husband sets down the drinks tray. Opens and pours the can of ginger ale into a tall glass with ice, inserts a straw, places it on the small table beside the chaise. "John," he asks, "will you do the honours?" He says this as if, except for the immediate and pressing errand of the highchair, he would sit right down and place the straw between Audrey's lips himself.

He never has, she thinks. He never will.

Even though Ted is almost a stranger to her now, Audrey knows that what she had with him, in the beginning and all through the kids growing up, everything, in fact, before the onset, was stronger, more passionate than what she sees that her daughter has settled for, or retreated to, with Douglas.

The first time she and Ted made love—before they were married, he said he needed it, and she wanted to be the thing he needed—he told her she was the only lover who hadn't made him feel dirty. She was shocked and hurt that he'd had others. For a while she'd worried he wouldn't want her, now that she was like all the rest. But then the whole of what he'd said sank in. Her saw her as his healthy angel, taking him away from a shuttered and unhappy house where his mother lay in bed most days, her illness unexplained, maybe unreal. His father's daily abdication—he came home late or not at all—was a source of pain and embarrassment to Ted. Audrey offered the one thing that could get him back from the place he went inside himself after being in that dingy house. The sex was always good. And the truth is, she'd have been happy to continue, but when she could no longer raise her pelvis too accommodate him, it affected his performance. "Like hugging up to a side of beef," he said petulantly—well, he was working in the restaurant business by then. She forgave him the spontaneous cruelty, but they never tried again.

What her son-in-law offers is the one thing Audrey can't give her girl, her boys; it's the one thing her husband never really managed, he with his business ventures, salesman first, then restaurant owner, the projects smaller and smaller, less and less ambitious. The bills mounted; money—unlike caterpillar tents—didn't grow on trees.

John and his girlfriend are arguing about what's best on a hamburger. Carrie's choice is ketchup and pepper only. He maintains an insistence on mustard and relish, oozing in a radioactive green from the edge of soft saucershaped buns. He makes up the first burger for Audrey, who sits at an odd angle on the orange-and-white woven netting of her chaise lounge, legs pale under her skirt, the lazy dark hairs that start at her ankles poking at the cotton. He has to feed her, small bites torn from the bun and meat. He teases her while he feeds her and she laughs, a long high whinny. She lacks the muscle strength to make the sound as full and fruity as she means it. She knows the teasing is to deflect attention from the slow cruel march of sclerosis around her body. Cell by cell, it consumes her, this living death. It has moved into her throat; even single words are an effort.

It's not so easy away from the hospital, she thinks, pretending in so many directions at once. She uses up all her available energy just lying in the chaise, being the perfect guest. Her eyes are on Teddie's stout arms hammering the plastic tray of his highchair. We're alike, she thinks, grandson and grandmother, what the disease has done to me he comes by naturally. People feed us, diaper our bottoms, put us in special seats, tuck us into bed earlier than we ever want to go. And he'll grow out of it.

Ten years have passed since the onset of a disease that has cannibalized her personality and her life. If she yearned after everything she'd lost she'd be empty. She has adjusted, she has learned that its progress through her body is of clinical interest. Sometimes, she even looks forward to the day she is not the woman anymore, but the full complement of altered cells at the very end of this long, drawn-out ending, when even oxygen is finally discarded.

She could never tell John this though he pushes her to talk, thinks it might lead somewhere, to his own and his brother's Buddhist beliefs, as if they might, by osmosis, soon be hers. He wants her to absorb spiritual acceptance. In her own way, she has already achieved it, and yet she loves her son's fervent and naive hope that he can offer something that belies where she is and what she has become.

Spiritual issues don't come up with her daughter or with Ted during his occasional half hour at the hospital, reciting newspaper headlines and offering anecdotes about a neighbour's dog, a shirt ripped by the drycleaners. For her husband, this wasting illness is the ultimate betrayal. She was supposed to be his buttress, a conduit of good energy in a house that was bright, clean, and full of laughter, which she offered, until her own internal structure began to disintegrate, until her muscles failed her, until sons, daughter, and husband were no longer within the circle of her loving arms.

"More salad, Mom?" John asks. No, she shakes her head slightly. Carrie and John rise, pick up bowls and jars and crumpled napkins, and carry them into the house.

Audrey is watching her son-in-law beside the apple tree and she is thinking: he has two problems in his backyard, those tent caterpillars and me. She watches as he lights a tightly rolled newspaper and then holds the torch aloft, touching fire to this and that cocoon, the translucent web alive with movement, caterpillars racing up their spun white walls, away from the flames. Disease is what he does at the clinic, not here in this neat and ordered backyard in this neighbourhood of blond brick houses. At work he could study an X-ray, consult a colleague, write a prescription, or order surgery. At work he could see her as a patient, a necessary statistic, one of a small percentage of people he cannot help.

She catches her daughter's eye, works to make her lips move in the direction of a smile.

"This is nice, sweetie," she says. "Thank you."

Donna pats her mother's arm, and her mother wonders again if the doctor-husband is a good and tender lover. Donna doesn't look unhappy.

John's girlfriend does. Carrie is an artist. In moments of discomfort such as this, her smile is as thin as skim milk, her pouty prettiness given over to a perched watchfulness, to sudden if interrupted movements. Today, she has already spilled a drink. It is obvious to Audrey that her son and his girlfriend are sleeping together and that this adds to, rather than diminishes, Carrie's insecurity.

John has been talking about a trip to Mexico. Audrey will miss him terribly, but she has been encouraging. He has not mentioned Carrie in his plans. Audrey suspects he needs to get away from the demands of his women.

"What's the delectable entree today Mrs. W?" John asks Mrs. Wilson, who complains incessantly about the food. "Slab of cow and heap of potato flake? A side dish of wilted lettuce? Jumbly Jell-O to top it all off?"

"Oh John," Mrs Wilson titters, "it's bad enough without you going on!" He walks around their hospital room bursting with health, a wise-cracking, gum-snapping ski bum, blond hair worn longish at the back and sometimes restrained by a trucker's cap or toque, which he sets at a rakish or ridiculous angle.

After every visit, he walks a few steps down the hall and then sneaks back and peeks around the door frame, stretching his arm straight up and flopping his hand twice, staccatowaving to his mother whose head is turned toward the door, waiting for this ritual exchange. He winks. With a lopsided grin, she tries to wink back. Usually she manages only to close her eyes. It's hard for her, a battle of will against sclerosis, but they both need to witness her efforts, the tiny goodbye a necessary torture for each of them. When it's done he leaves and she turns her gaze back toward the

TV that he'd switched on before he left.

Occasionally, he brings Carrie, who stoops for the obligatory kiss then sits, awkwardly, in a vinyl hospital chair, trying to be a good sport, trying to smile and participate in the conversation, eyes skittering off the four beds and the four sick ladies, eyes returning again and again to Audrey's son, wanting what he can't give. Audrey hurts for her, a little. What must it be like when "the other woman" is your lover's pale prone mother, waiting for death in an ugly hospital overlooking the Don Valley Parkway?

Almost everything that is any good in John, Audrey knows, comes to her or is spewed up in a shower of dry snow, small sparkling cascades propelled outward from the edges of his skis on the hill behind Silverwoods, the large dairy manufacturer overlooking the valley, where the Parkway flows beneath Lawrence Ave.

The ski hill. She pictures him there. Long days of lying still in a hospital bed, nothing to fill them but the imagined itineraries of her children: Ben's mountains and meditations—these are the hardest because she's never been overseas; Donna's routines with Teddie; and John delivering the mail or on his beloved skis. She used to take the kids when they were younger, when she could snap her own boots into bindings and fly down the hills. She can still remember that, the clean smell of winter and the dry swift sounds of waxed wood on packed snow. She often closes her eyes and sees, not just John, but her own ski tips fluttering over divots on a steep white slope.

It's eight now; he won't come in off the hills until they close up at ten, stopping the lifts, turning off the lights around the rental shack and the snack bar. But even then some of the tow guys might have a case of twelve under the shed in the snow. Even then the lights on the slopes burn all night. If he's up for it he might side-step up the hill and take a last run, a little drunk, attempting and accomplishing a spread-eagle off the big bump in the middle of number two, skiing like a mad man, Hot Dog Sutherland, king of the slopes. He'll yodel into the night, and his friends at the bottom will call out his name, they'll clap and whistle, it's the greatest show in the suburbs, an hour before midnight at the Don Valley Ski Hill.

"Damn," he's just remembered that Carrie wanted him to call. The T-bar tugs him up the white slope. The girls in the snack bar will let him use the phone. Maybe after a few runs.

Under an indigo sky he pushes off, slides in a long arc until of their own accord his skis find the mogul, nothing fancy, just a little blip and jump, the familiar thrill for the second or two that he's airborne and a perfect landing. He doesn't think when he's skiing, his body knows what to do all by itself.

"Audrey?"

One of the aides, Rita, is standing beside the bed, her plump brown face opening into a smile, her hand on Audrey's shoulder. Waking, Audrey feels she is coming down from the clouds, sliding too fast out of the wide silvery place in which she was flying, bird shapes advancing and receding, her own wings pumping to keep her aloft. For a moment she panics, "Am I falling?" and the little flat gasp taken into her lungs brings hospital air, the knowledge of gravity, and the awareness of her body like a slab sheathed with pale green sheets.

The best dreams are the hardest to leave. She stops flying.

"Someone's here to see you," Rita says. She is holding a wash cloth up to Audrey's face. The cloth presses gently against one cheek, a cleaning swipe. I'm drooling, Audrey thinks. Before Rita leaves she cranks the bed up a few notches, arranges the blanket at the side, bending to check, making sure the urine bag doesn't show.

Must be someone new, thinks Audrey.

It's Gaetan—John's friend. The boys met on a language-exchange in junior high. Gaetan came back a few times after that first official visit; he and John had a bond. She remembered that he liked her macaroni and cheese, but hated mustard on his sandwiches.

John's at work. Gaetan has a train to catch in a few hours.

She smiles her weak smile at him, listens as he tells her about his mother, his work with street kids, the girlfriend he plans to marry. He holds a photo of the young woman up and angles it so that Audrey can see.

"I'm going to teach her to make the *nouilles au fromage*, like you do," he says. The simple fact that he has neglected to use the past tense makes tears spring to her eyes.

"Oh Audrey, I do not want to make you cry."

This is the hardest thing, she thinks, that she can no longer raise her own hands to cover her face. That crying has become a public act.

"No," she says, "it's not you," and she forces her lips to move upward in another smile. He is a brave boy to come here on his own and shows none of the discomfort that outsiders often display. But Gaetan has a life and plans. For John everything is on hold.

"Do you still ski?" Audrey asks after she has composed herself.

"Oh yes, Audrey, every weekend in winter, but I was never as good as John. He could have represented this country at the Winter Olympics."

After Gaetan leaves, bending to kiss her pale forehead, Audrey says no to lunch and asks Rita to pull the curtains around her bed. She needs the pretence of privacy. Some things still need to be mourned.

An evening eight years or so earlier, before she was hospitalized, John came in the door and seeing her, blurted out what had obviously carried him on a cloud all the way home: "Mackie asked to see me in his office today." Audrey knew he was referring to the head of the high school phys-ed department, Mr McElwaine. "He thinks I could train for the Olympics."

"Oh honey," she'd said, trying to rise out of her wheelchair, hand slipping off the armrest, body sliding forward, just missing a complete fall because John was suddenly there on his knee in front of her.

"Mom, what are you doing?!" he asked, lifting her back onto the seat, rearranging her legs.

"I wanted to hug you, John, "she said." I'm so proud."

"Ah Mom, it's a compliment, but it's not … I don't really want to do it that bad."

He'd walked into the kitchen, whistling, suggesting tea, and it was then that she understood.

John did the shopping with his dad. Ben did the laundry and his sister cooked, the cleaning was shared by all of them. Her medical bills were gaining on them.

She couldn't hold a cup in her hands anymore. Not even a cup of tea.

A woman knows her husband. Even when she no longer shares his bed she knows him that way.

Olivia is from Jamaica, a single mother of two grown daughters still back home, and John likes her; it is clear by the way he says her name when he finally admits to her existence. Audrey does not tell her son that this is a relief. There's little left that she can do, but she fervently hopes that they'll get what they need, that they'll be okay without her. Ben is seeking transcendence in Nepal. Donna has settled for something else in Oakville. John is the witness, holding on to what is left of their family, shielding it and her as she once held them all. He's like his father but so much stronger. For Ted, it's simple: he needs warm and comforting arms, the good physical act of love and release. His massive heart attack takes everyone by surprise;

how could fate do that, take him first and so soon? All his life running from the ill health of others only to be tripped up and taken out of the race by his own funky heart.

At the chapel, protocol puts Audrey, in her wheelchair, at the front, close to the coffin. Mother of his children. Wife. She can no longer turn her own head and has to wait until the service is over. It takes all her strength just to hiss the request, "Turn me around." It's not the reaction John expected. Tears maybe?

A moment later, he still hasn't moved. She's angry now. "*Turn me*, John."

He releases her brakes and wheels the chair around. Audrey notes the quiet style. Olivia's legs are slim and straight beneath the good wool of a navy suit, burgundy silk folded at her neck. Streaks of grey in straightened hair beneath a smart hat. Audrey wants to say: I always knew, it doesn't matter, I'm glad you came. But the funeral and the fight with her son and life, yes—what is left of it after the disease has siphoned off its ever-increasing share—has drained her. And just at this moment, at the end of her husband's funeral, no words remain.

"John?"

"Ya?" He's flipping through the paper for the article he wants to read her.

She swallows. "I want to go skiing."

He goes still.

She continues, taking a breath, as deep as she's capable, "You leave in two months. I want to do something before ..." and that's all she can manage.

He runs a hand over his face. Sighs. "Okay," he says.

She is suddenly afraid that she is asking too much. But he is speaking again, with more enthusiasm. "I saw this thing called a "pulk," on TV a while ago. From Norway. Kid in it was a paraplegic, but he had two short poles and man," he's nodding his head, looking into the middle distance, a smile on his face," could that thing go."

And because he now has a way to atone for his impending desertion, he makes it happen.

On the big day the nurses manage to get her into a pair of oversize ski-pants, a turtleneck, and a large warm cardigan. They wrap an extra blanket around her legs. John brings in an old navy blue ski jacket. It isn't until he puts it over her shoulders that she catches a whiff, stale and yet familiar—Old Spice—and realizes the jacket used to be Ted's.

John's buddies have gathered at the ski hill. They've got a silly toque for her head, and to fit over her hands, fingers folded in paralysis like little wings, a pair of big leather mitts. They lay a sheet of thin foam on two sleds that have been bolted together.

She's strapped into it. Someone wiggles a pillow under her head and shoulders so that she can see where she's going.

The guy at the controls of the T-bar promises to take it nice and slow. John and a buddy are holding onto straps attached to the side of the sled. They're going to drag her up as the tow pulls them; a third boy is in front and a fourth behind. Several times they stop, either because her runners stick or because John or his friend is pulled off his bar. Each time, one of the guys skis downhill of Audrey and plants his poles in the snow at her feet, to prevent the sled from losing ground. In this fashion, bumping forward in increments, they make it to the top of the hill.

"We're going to ski in a pack, Mom," John says. And she knows that he means, "Just in case."

Audrey, on her back, looks up past arms and legs to pale sky. She hears the rustling of nylon against nylon, the slight crunch and sucking sound of poles digging in and out of snow as they slide toward the crest and stop.

"Everybody ready?" John asks. Straps creak and wood rubs against metal beneath her and with a gentle lurch, they've begun. The boys, snow ploughing, mutter instructions to each other, "slower" or "to the left" and their breath puffs out in small clouds. The first run is over before she realizes, and she wants it again, the slow hiss of her runners and their skis on hard-packed snow, the rippling movement beneath her back, buttocks, and thighs.

John and his friends exchange high fives: the double sled wasn't such a dopey idea after all. The next tow ride is a little faster, and soon they are taking longer runs and wider curves, a little more speed, a tiny mogul or two. And her body lying down remembers her body standing up, curving, dipping, following the rhythms of snow and air and speed.

On their seventh or eighth run—Audrey has lost count—it begins to snow. Big flakes drift toward her blinking eyes like tiny grey moths, the snowflakes darker than the silver sky. They catch on her eyelashes and Audrey opens her mouth, sticks out her tongue and tastes snow.

Someone asks her if she wants to stop.

"Oh no," she says. After all, what's a little weather? What's a little real weather?

Let's take the Parkway, people say, to the theatre or the Eaton Centre, to jobs in the city's core. And young kids heading downtown in a car on halfday loan from somebody's parents, see it as the drive towards something more exciting, away from suburban boredom, green lawns, and full fridges. But for John, the DVP is always the long drive to his mother's bed, a way station in this long journey of death by degrees.

"I can't explain it," he says now. "Even when someone is stripped of everything, they can still give. I wasn't doing all that much for her. It was the other way around."

After too long a wait, too long a sojourn in a hospital room—whose windows, if she had been able to walk over to them, would have provided her with a wide view of the valley—she dies.

North of the room she occupied for over a decade is a defunct ski hill, its owners long bankrupt. The young stars and the muscular boys—operators of tows, earners of skipatrol badges—have drifted into marriages and jobs. The snack bar and rental shack are gone, torn down a few years after the property was ceded back to the city. But the frames for the rope tows and T-bar remain. Memory can still be tugged uphill. Lamps which shone on the last run of the night every winter night for years, now void of electricity, would, by the light of remembering, reveal the curving descent of a teenager old before his time, too burdened, but in his own words, "blessed." Beneath a blue-black sky. Cutting perfect curves in blue-white snow.

In the Drink

1962

"It's from the 20s. One of those old silent films, very jerky. Hah! The gal's making love to a donkey, right? He's *huge*."

Peepo makes a fist, holds his arm out and pumps it three times, then leans toward the fire and stirs it with a stick.

"Careful of the flames. Wouldn't want to singe the eyebrow," Frank says. Peepo gets his name from peering out beneath his shaggy and almost continual eyebrows. At least this is the story he favours; others say it's because of peepholes he drills into the women's change rooms of the department store where he works.

Peepo sits back, continues on with his story. "Lifts her legs right off the floor. In the next scene she's giving the animal a blow job."

He picks up the beer bottle at his side, places his thumb over the mouth and shakes it.

"Guess what happens next."

Kind and a little innocent, Moony is the only one to take the bait, "What?"

Peepo takes a swig from the bottle and lets out a long gargling yodel. Beer flows over his lips and chin. Moony pulls back fast. But he can't stop staring, just like he can't stop his brain from interpreting the subsiding foam.

"Oh," says Moony.

"*O* is right." Peepo laughs, bending to wipe his mouth with his t-shirt.

"Where do you see that stuff?" asks Dirk. Not for the first time, he is wondering why this annual camping trip—the men met a decade ago, volunteering to rebuild a library badly damaged after a fire—now seems to include this interloper. Peepo was not one of the original group. He is a neighbour of Moony's. And Moony just can't say no.

"Not where, *why*?" says Frank.

"There's this other one, with a snake."

"Keep it to yourself," says Frank, heading down to the rocky shoreline of the campsite.

Peepo sneers and grabs at his crotch. "You said it, man: my python. My cobra."

Dirk rolls his eyes and follows after Frank.

"What's the matter with you guys? You wanna hear it J.B., eh? Buddy?"

J.B. and the dog curled at his feet rise. They walk down to the granite shelf sloping into the lake where the other men talk, backs to the campfire.

"Christ, what a bunch of old farts," mutters Peepo. "It's just you and me, Moon."

2003

As always, they were resisting. Tim knelt in one corner of his impossible room, a disaster of action figures splayed on the blue rug, constructing an addition to his already impenetrable Lego fortress. He was making the noises he liked to make: walkie-talkie static, distant explosions, the soft pop of bullets from a silencer. So much for peaceful toys, Rina thought, emptying the laundry hamper in the hall into a basket. She could hear the tinny buzz of a Walkman from the washroom. A glance through the doorway revealed, simultaneously, three Courtneys, the real girl and her two reflections, a huddle of young faces intent on a search for minuscule imperfections. Rina took in the hip-huggers and a snug t-shirt that cleared her daughter's perfect tummy.

"That's a lot of flesh sweetheart. You'll have to change." She said it loud enough to penetrate the music then automatically mimicked her daughter's sour grimace. "Yes, you *have* to." Upstairs again after starting the washing machine, Rina stopped in her son's doorway. "Five minutes to take off, Timmy. Where's the card you made Gramps?"

A Lego rocket launcher swivelled, let fire. The small projectile bounced off the bedside lamp and skittered across the folded construction paper beneath it. "Happy Birthday Gramps," it said, purple crayon on red, three sparkly stickers.

"That's great. Pack up some toys. We're taking a cake."

"What kind?"

"Carrot."

"That's for old people."

"Yes, honey, for Gramps." Who wasn't all that old, chronologically speaking. Except that to the kids anyone past forty was ancient. Rina moved on to the master bedroom. In front of her own mirror, she pushed her hand through growing-out streaks of honey blond then placed her fingertips at her temples and stretched the skin until the crow's feet disappeared. Mascara? Courtney wears enough for both of us, she thought. For her, these Sunday visits were a given, a pledge of love and loyalty to the man she'd married; Hugh believed his father was kept if not alert, then at least alive, by the regular company of family and friends.

Long ago, she'd asked Hugh about the name. "He was christened Timothy Douglas, but no-one ever called him that. It was 'that moon-faced boy,' and then just 'Moony.'" The strange name stuck, although Moony shed the baby fat. He was almost handsome when he entered adulthood, his eager face bending to his pretty bride. Rina had seen the pictures, early black and whites and then others, various permutations and arrangements of two women: Kate and her mother and three kids around an easy chair in which sat—or slumped—the man who was Hugh's father but whom Hugh has never known as a functioning adult. "It stunned me, when I went to school, to see that other kids had fathers who *did* things."

Hugh still talked to his father, long earnest monologues about whatever he was doing at work or home. But Rina had not so much decided on as fallen into a different pattern. After she'd gone through Moony's drawers and made a note of the underwear, hankies, and socks that needed replacing, after she'd watered the three African violets and straightened the pictures on his wall, Rina sat with the old man and held his hand, stroking the raised veins and coarse white hairs, just sat and watched out the window, too. Whatever was going on inside that white head of his, projected on various blue or pewter skies, that was Moony's reality, and all she could wish for was that he either liked what he saw or, conversely, that if it was the screen for replaying long-ago hurts, an old person's ever-remembered youthful shame, that one day it might pain him less. Some of his cronies still came by. Dirk walked with the aid of a walker, but he was such a charmer he made Rina feel as pretty as Courtney. Frank, solid and tenacious as an oak, smelled of wood smoke and sometimes the coffee he'd just had at Tim Horton's. He didn't say much, but his presence seemed to reassure Moony.

There had been an accident in Moony's twenties, two in fact; Moony was witness to a friend's drowning death and then almost drowned, himself, the next year. Frank and Dirk had been there both times, in fact, they'd probably saved Moony, breathing life into his lungs, pumping out the awesome quantity of lake that he'd inhaled or swallowed. But he'd been "on the other side" long enough to come back changed, not completely addled, but spacey and easily tired. His children, just toddlers at the time of the accident, were fortunate in their mother, who worked her way up through a Sarnia company until she was an assistant manager. She died of a brain aneurism at her desk, at the age of fifty-two.

"I didn't think he'd outlive her," said Hugh. "She never considered shipping him off to an institution. But I think there might have been a lover. I hope so. I mean, she was so …" He opened his hands like a blooming flower. "You know."

Yes, she did know. It was how Rina felt with him—alive, engaged, *connected*. She never questioned her choice of mate, though it meant having an old shambling man in the house for the first two years of their marriage, until a series of small strokes landed him in the nursing home.

At least it was a good one, and Moony had his loyal entourage of visitors, the hale administering to the feeble. And Rina, careful not to let nicknames attach themselves to her kids, thought Hugh's father had finally and completely grown into his name: Moony *was* moony, now. He hung on their horizon, passing through his phases of somnambulance and lucidity. But Rina found it harder and harder to get the kids' butts in gear for the weekly pilgrimage.

"Courtney, Tim, c'mon."

"Mom, can I …"

"It's his birthday, Courtney, so whatever you're asking to do instead, no."

"You don't even know what I'm gonna say."

Surely to God Rina had never curled her lip that way at her own mother. "What?"

"Can I go to Nadia's *on the way home*?"

"Fine, but change that top. C'mon Timmy."

1963

It was the weekend they looked forward to all year: five guys, three nights, two canoes and a kayak, thirty-six beers—not much but still an accomplishment, considering the long portages into Macintosh Lake—and uncounted ounces of hard stuff decanted into plastic containers and wineskins. It was a matter of pride that they never ran out. On the third night, just when it seemed that the last drop had been drunk, one of the men would slip back into the tent, dig around in his knapsack and come out with another mickey. They had three two-man tents and all the fishing gear, plus a pack stuffed full of food: rice, instant mashed potatoes, Frank's homemade beef jerky, various condiments, a tub of lard, packages of Tang and Nabob coffee, bacon, eggs in yellow plastic carriers, and biscuit mix. Margaret, Dirk's wife, always insisted on packing a cooler bag with raw vegetables and fruit. After a roadside stop for burgers and fries—two burgers and a large fries for Dirk—they drove to the Algonquin Park office, their last stop before driving down a dirt road to the wharf where they'd launch. Dirk pawed through the cooler bag before going alone into the office. It was his job to pay for the permit and parking. He smiled at the woman behind the counter. Tubby he might be, but still a charmer. She smiled back. He placed two plastic bags of vegetables on the counter.

"My wife wants me to stick with my regime," he looked rueful. "But it's my weekend with the boys. Please take this."

"Are you sure?" she asked.

"You're doing me a favour," he winked as he swung out through the screen door. He'd kept the peppers and onions for frying with the sausages and the fish they hoped to catch, and he kept the parsley because last year Frank had hooked a big bass by adding a sprig of it to his line.

Their camping mood was boyish camaraderie soon to be mixed with beer bravado. It was a Friday in August. They'd all asked for two days off work to make it a long weekend, that is all except Moony, whose good humour was not entirely authentic. He'd been laid off of the afternoon shift at the factory a few weeks earlier, a development he'd managed to keep secret so far, even from Kate. He'd take the dinner she packed him and leave the house at three thirty and head off in the usual direction, but instead of turning in at the factory gates he'd keep on driving right out of town. He spent the afternoons tramping in the woods, or if it rained, in the library of a nearby town, then ate his meal in the car and stopped at one of the highway taverns to nurse a beer and watch whatever game was playing on the TV over the bar, timing his arrival home so that it coincided with all the nights he'd been gainfully employed. August's rent was covered. There was enough in the bank to last through fall. But then it would be winter and Katie was expecting their third child. The idea of the camping weekend had kept him going, as had the hope that one of the guys might be able to suggest something or get him on where they worked. He could have asked them earlier, but he didn't want to worry Kate during the pregnancy, and if he'd dropped by to speak to one of the men at home after their workday then Dirk's wife or Frank's might have wondered out loud to Kate and, heck, it just seemed simpler, all around, to wait for the three uninterrupted days in the park.

They'd all been up since sparrow fart, meeting at the burger joint for their caloric "brunch" because, of course, they'd burn it all off in the paddling and portaging ahead. They wanted to arrive at Macintosh Lake well before any other campers descended. Monday was their day to get home and get over what by then would be massive hangovers. The rest of the weekend would be a case of the hair of the dog that bit them.

On the subject of dogs this was their first trip without one. In the past J.B. had brought Rowdy, who, despite her name, tended to sit quietly in the bow and carried her own dog food and bowl in a set of saddle bags that J.B.'s wife had sewn before she died. Rowdy was curious but careful around the flopping fish that landed in the bottom of the canoe. The only one who could tolerate J.B.'s snoring, she slept in his tent. She licked the frying pan clean, which had grossed Peepo out until Dirk commented that a dog's mouth was about a hundred times cleaner than a man's. Back in high school Peepo had gotten into a brawl over a girl, biting the other guy's earlobe clean through and narrowly missing a jail term for it. So he'd tolerated Rowdy's tongue bath on the skillet, but he always gave it a good scrubbing afterwards.

There was some discussion about whether the dog's presence might protect them from bears, a view contested by Frank, who, though he genuinely liked Rowdy, felt that having pets on camping trips was just asking for trouble. Rowdy had been hit by a car last winter and ended up with a gimpy leg. The vet who had examined her decided the matter, advising J.B. to leave her in his care for the time being. As they launched their boats, J.B. said, "I miss my dog," a statement that gave Moony the shivers. He was recalling something from the year before. Waking with an urge to pee, he'd crawled out of his tent and padded in bare feet to the edge of the clearing. This put him closer to J.B.'s tent, tucked away in an alcove surrounded by trees. The others always agreed to let J.B. put his tent there because of his snoring. But what Moony heard that night wasn't catarrh, it was an unmistakable rhythm that culminated in a quick high yip. By next morning Moony couldn't be sure he hadn't dreamt it.

There was an enormous load to cram into the two canoes. They roped the tents and tarp onto the kayak. No sooner was he settled in one of the canoes than Frank said, "Sun's over the yard arm," and rhythmically whacked the caps off five beers against the gunnels.

By the time they got to Macintosh, they were all a little pickled. The sun was high and hot. They set up camp on their favourite site, unloading the gear and sticking a cooler and the beers in the water. Dirk wanted to get the tents up but J.B. argued that the sun would move and what was in the shade now wouldn't be later. He didn't want his brand new nylon Eureka exposed to damaging UV rays. This sounded like a load of hooey to Peepo who had invited himself along two years earlier after hearing about the trip from Moony. Peepo was still a novice camper, along more for the drinking and a captive audience than to smell the pines and hear the loons. But Dirk conceded. "J.B.'s right. Let's go for a swim first.

A pair of ravens cronked as they flew overhead and disappeared beyond the thick bush of the eastern shore of the lake. A thick press of cedar at the water's edge gave way to red and then white pines, puffy sleeves reaching toward the almost cloudless sky. The slight breeze ruffled the surface of the water and created a band of molten silver daubs.

They stripped off their sweaty t-shirts and shorts—none of them bothered with swim trunks—and stepped or dove into the water. They were soon splashing around, spitting water, yahooing with the exuberance of kids. Frank, a strong swimmer, struck out across to the big island, some metres distant. The others soon tired of swimming, except for Peepo, who had waited till after blowing up his air mattress. He was floating on it naked in the sun while Moony, J.B., and Dirk sat on the granite shelf at the water's edge, drinking the last of the beers.

"Look at that," Dirk said.

"What?" Moony said. He'd been absorbed in the lake's reflection of the sky, the way the ripples from Peepo's raft broke the reflection of one white cloud into dozens of mini clouds.

"The cheeky bugger," said Dirk. He was looking into the water.

"You mean Frank?" J.B. pointed to where Frank stood on the opposite shore.

Moony held out his arm and sighted along it like an artist. "He's the size of my thumb."

"The measure of a man is not the size of his willy," said Dirk, "but what he does with it."

Moony began to blush. "I wasn't looking at … I wasn't measuring his …"

"Moony, I'm joking, son," Dirk said, surprised to see tears forming in the younger man's eyes. He'd take him out in the canoe later, for a little chat. "I was talking about the bass."

The others had to squint and refocus to see what was happening beneath the lake's surface. But there it was, a big fish checking out their underwater larder.

"Where'd he go?" It was Peepo, sitting up, his legs straddling the now

V-shaped rubber mattress. He was staring at the spot where Frank had been standing a moment earlier.

"You know Frank," said Dirk. "He likes to explore."

"Takin' a dump more like it," said Peepo.

"You weren't planning to save yours in a jar, were you?" asked Dirk.

"No, but I go here." He meant the site's boom box. "What's he gonna use for bum wad?"

"Leaves, probably."

"Hope he doesn't pick any poison ivy."

"I think you can count on Frank to know his poisonous plants," said J.B. dryly.

But Peepo wasn't listening. He mock-wrestled with the wedge of air mattress between his legs. "Oh man, look at the size of it!" He grinned at the men.

"C'mon boys," said Dirk. "Let's go catch ourselves some dinner."

They took the canoes out and fished as the sun dipped lower in the sky. After an hour they were back, cleaning their catch, starting the fire, putting up tents, their campsite a hub of activity crisscrossed with purposeful strides. It didn't hurt that they'd taken a break from beer—mainly because they'd drunk it all—and were waiting till after dinner to start on the hard stuff.

The hard stuff. Maybe the hardest stuff of all is recognizing that you've gone too far, three liquor-laden, testosterone-laced days that culminate in something not just dumb but tragic.

Frank would blame himself because he'd gone for a walk—more like a bush-whack—along the shore. It was a moonlit night. Clear, the lake like glass.

J.B. wouldn't blame himself but would drink himself into the grave. Rigidity and loneliness, that and knowing—maybe not consciously but on that other level, the old man's bitter subconscious — that he'd been a brute to his wife and estranged son. Not to mention cirrhosis of the liver and perhaps—was he in denial about that, too?—the shame of screwing his dog. A secret he'd have taken to his grave. Except that Moony knew, though Moony, being who he was before the accident, wasn't sure what he knew and later, would more or less lose the capacity to comment. The vet had examined the dog and done a swab which revealed human sperm in her vagina. He told J.B. to leave the dog at the kennel and then lied and said she died of an embolism, a delayed result of her earlier collision with a car. The ashes he gave J.B. were those of a young, collarless bitch hit by a transport truck on the highway. The vet liked animals more than people, and he didn't think Rowdy's job in life was to service her owner. He found her a new home in Toronto and drove her down. Rowdy seemed to recognize a good thing when she found it and, under the care of her new family, lived to a fine old canine age. She would retain the tendency to shy away when someone patted her bum. Her former owner, who would predecease her by some years, never got over the loss.

Dirk, in the way of good men everywhere, blamed himself. Christian charity—give the guy another chance—had overridden his common sense. Peepo had been weird the first year and barely tolerable the second. But Dirk believed in God and the Holy Trinity. He believed in the mathematical logic of baseball and abided by its rules. This was Peepo's third and final—nobody knew just how final—turn at bat. The older men simply avoided him and so he got paired with Moony a lot, because Moony was quiet enough not to complain.

Moony was dozing by the fire when Peepo punched his arm and suggested they take a canoe out. The two of them paddled out under the light of a seven-eighths moon. Moony would say—and it would be true—that he was too drunk to remember exactly what took place. He could recall the sudden bounce of the canoe, but then several things happened at once: a lurch and what sounded like things hitting the sides, Peepo's startled "Whooaaaoooo," which, if he hadn't died, would have been comical, a cartoon swoop of noise ending in a big sloppy splash. During it all, Moony, trying to keep his balance, lunged backwards to counter his forward momentum and went toppling overboard. He was underwater for no more than a few seconds, but he swallowed water and came up blustering. Dirk, hearing the commotion, yelled at him to "Hold on, for God's sake we're coming!" while he and J.B. scrambled to the remaining canoe and paddled hard to reach a spluttering Moony. Frank came back on the run, kicking off his shoes, dropping his pants and shucking his shirt before executing a perfect stride-jump into the water and swimming in powerful strokes to the two canoes. He dove, over and over, amazed at his own lucidity, feeling almost superhuman but sadly not endowed with the underwater night-vision required. While he searched in vain for Peepo, Dirk and J.B. managed to haul a gasping Moony into their canoe.

The official, if well-lubricated, story was this: Peepo, in characteristic fashion, had attempted the outlandish, gunnel bobbing on his own dare. But he'd slipped and gone over the side, banging his head either on the canoe or on the large underwater boulder. It was a glacial erratic, dropped by retreating ice several million years earlier. Frank knew of its presence because he'd been swimming with his eyes open breast-stroke, looking down; he'd seen the boulder and dropped a foot down to touch it. He'd idly considered stopping, turning and waving at the rest of them, but he was determined to log his swimming miles, and so he swam over the boulder six times before Peepo's head hit it. The only way that Peepo's head could have hit it was for him to fall out of the canoe head-first and, as fate would have it, at a fairly precise angle. On impact, Peepo probably experienced a last spasm of light as various orifices opened: nasal passages rapidly filling with water, sphincter expelling a single turd, and his bladder releasing the by-now-processed liquor he'd consumed. Moony would have fallen into the lake right after, and as he floundered backwards, he must have absorbed, through the rippling water, Peepo's final juddering moment of consciousness.

The weekend which had started so well had come to this: uncounted—but not un-drunk—ounces of hard stuff, thirty-six beers consumed quickly and pissed away, two canoes, a kayak, three nights, four guys, and a body that, immediately after the accident, they couldn't find. They tried, but they were all stupid with alcohol and shock. Frank dove for over an hour before fatigue made him give up. Dirk and J.B. held the second canoe steady while Frank swung his leg up and over the side, and they all paddled back to shore where, out of a need for mental medication or just to get through the night, they drank. They drank till everything was gone. They even found Peepo's bourbon, but the drinking they did after the accident only had the effect of making them feel more sober. None of them would get any rest that night, except for their missing campmate, who, like Luca Brasi in *The Godfather,* was "sleeping with the fish."

They took the canoes out the next morning. The body had floated farther than they'd imagined it could. Frank tied the rope around and under Peepo's trunk and under his arms and was the first to see that the fish had already had a go at the eyes. A question flashed through his mind, more in keeping with the dead man's preoccupations than his own: what might they have nibbled if the body had been naked? He hauled himself back into the canoe, and he and Dirk towed Peepo back to shore. They removed his sodden clothes. Moony lurched away to vomit when they found the waterlogged turd. They thought briefly about dry jeans and a t-shirt, but the body had changed with its overnight soaking. They wrapped Peepo in a tarp and laid him in the bottom of the canoe before setting out, hang dog, hung-over, and burdened by their temporary bier.

It was a long journey home.

And though Dirk's guilt would eventually be woven into the common-sense fabric of his life, i.e. accidents *happen;* though Frank would add the incident to an already cynical world-view; and though J.B. would hardly remember it except as an event peripheral to his own brooding; Moony would be branded by it for life.

A man is said to be responsible for the soul of the person he saves. But what is his connection to the one he doesn't save? Moony went into a fugue of depression that lasted into the winter. When Kate, nursing a newborn and caring for two toddlers, realized what they were up against—no money coming in and a despondent husband—she called her mother and her brother, two difficult calls. In February her brother came in his truck and drove them back to Sarnia, a place Kate had hoped never to return. After a few months, Moony found work in another factory, but was almost immediately laid off. Kate waited until the baby was partially weaned. Then, leaving her mother with enough formula for the afternoon feedings, she started working at a synthetic rubber manufacturer as a secretary to the manager, one Fred Beeker, who was attracted to her prettiness and her aura of preoccupied determination. Beeker had married his high school sweetheart, but they'd grown in divergent ways. He spent several mornings a week schlepping his son to hockey practice and tended to fall asleep in front of the TV at night. The rare sex the couple had happened in the dark and after both of them had consumed enough, in his case, beer, in hers, gin, to arouse a memory of passion. He was stunned to hear that Kate had three young ones at home. The sight of her trim legs and the line of her bottom through her fitted skirt both unnerved him and became a daily necessity.

Kate was unaware of the effect she had on her boss. She was concentrating on Moony. Moony was a mess. Kate loved him deeply and because of that, was able to see he couldn't help it. These were the days before therapy was *de rigueur*. When Kate asked her family doctor for help—now there was an old fart—he wrote out a prescription. And then Dirk, who was checking in on a monthly basis, called and suggested another camping trip.

"You've got to be kidding!?" she whispered into the phone. Not only did she hide these calls from Moony, she didn't want the children to overhear.

"No, Katie, I'm not. Think of it as getting back in the saddle."

Odd logic, but it might work. "Who will go?"

"Frank, me. J.B. I think it's best if it's as much like before as possible."

They were silent for a moment, remembering Peepo. And then Kate sighed and said maybe Moony needed "a good shaking up. But, you'll take care of him," she said, "won't you?"

Kate assumed that she and Dirk were speaking the same language. She didn't bother to tell Dirk about Moony's meds because, though the doctor had warned Moony, he hadn't warned Kate that alcohol in large amounts could potentiate the effect of the anti-depressants. For a man like Dirk, the idea of "taking care" meant getting your buddy drunk at the appropriate times. Those were when his girlfriend dumped him; the night before his wedding; when his wife gave birth; when he received a promotion; lost a job; or slipped into a funk. And Moony had slipped deeper than a standard funk.

At the time, Kate and her boss were in the same boat. Kate hadn't felt like having sex at the end of her pregnancy, nor was she much in the mood for it in the early months of nursing. As well as sore breasts and a tender vagina, there was her growing anxiety about money. But even after they moved to Sarnia and she pulled their financial life back in some sort of balance, Moony no longer turned to her at night. She tried in her sweet way, to seduce him, without success. Perhaps it came from being so pretty, a woman with a face that attracted others and made them smile, but Kate was essentially an optimist. She thought Moony would get back on track or, as Dirk put it, "back in the saddle."

She took Moony to the bus on the Wednesday before the camping weekend and said goodbye with a big hug and a twinge of something like relief. On Thursday, Fred Beeker told her he'd need her to accompany him off-site the next day, and Kate queried neither their destination nor the purpose of their trip. His clipped request had come across as a necessity, if not quite a demand.

He had suggested a picnic en route and so Kate didn't question the blanket he pulled out of his car when they stopped. She was outside on a summer day when she was supposed to be working, feeling a giddy and only slightly guilty sense of freedom because her husband was otherwise occupied for four days. The kids were fine. The sun on her shoulders felt sublime. Besides the delicious odour from the chicken and rolls she had baked and brought, there was that clean, clear smell off the lake. She was momentarily carefree. She wanted to lie back and close her eyes, but she wasn't sure of the etiquette.

"Should I get my steno pad? It's in the car."

"Oh no, we can just relax." He didn't sound very relaxed. His lips were pressed together now and his face was slightly flushed. She kicked her shoes off and lay back on the blanket.

"Kate," he said. It came out a groan.

Shielding her eyes with her hand, she turned to look at him. She was calm and happy. She was open as an egg, sunny-side up. Later she wouldn't be sure who made the first move. Maybe she did. Maybe reaching out to troubled men had become automatic, but once it began it wasn't something she wanted to stop, a body could get—hers was—ravenous for this rhythm, this *fit*. As the baby seeks the breast, as the child seeks the hand and hug, two adult bodies sometimes seek each other out for reassurance, to be reminded that they are still alive, reaching for that other hungry animal underneath the soft armour of clothing, underneath careful human skin. A stranger. But not so strange.

She and Moony had never made love outside and now they never would. The second accident would be the result of Moony's first epileptic fit and that would be the result of too much alcohol in conjunction with a mild drug overdose which was the result of Moony being away from home and the watchful eye of his mother-in-law. He was vague about his own pill-taking regimen; had he taken his morning dose? Unsure, he took two with dinner and then let Dirk ply him with booze around the campfire all evening long. Eventually the others went to bed, leaving him by the fire: every once in a while a man needed to stay up later than his buddies to watch the flames die down to embers; there was the generic belief that this was good for the soul, and it simply didn't cross the brain pans of Frank, Dirk, or J.B. that Moony was suffering from an amnesiac and potentially suicidal sense of culpability. Moony still couldn't remember what had occurred immediately before Peepo's drowning, but he suspected it was bad. Now, by virtue of being seriously stoned for the first time in his life, he moved in slow-mo toward the small gravel and mud beach where they'd left the canoes. He watched himself turn over the red one, get into it and paddle out to a beckoning sparkle, a tossed gauntlet laid down by the moon and leading, surely, to those crucial five minutes. And then in the course of the petit mal seizure he had, Moony slipped forward. But fortunately he was way ahead of himself, what he'd seen in his imagination hadn't happened yet: he was still on shore. The others got to him after being woken by the sound, a kind of weird flapping, Moony's arms and legs against the overturned canoes. But Moony's head was dipping in and out of the water, and this is what almost killed him.

2003

Lately, his older sister has become a kind of alien. Once a month she gets what their mom calls "her period," a condition which confused Tim at first; he thought they meant the punctuation mark and wondered if she was carrying around a big black dot, although she didn't wear it on her forehead like Mrs. Ramamurthy next door. When he'd asked their mother about this she'd done that thing with her fingers at the side of her mouth which meant that he'd said something "cute," and then she'd explained the horrible truth. He couldn't believe it didn't hurt; certainly Courtney made a big deal of it, moaning on the couch and hogging the TV remote. She was getting zits, too, and Timmy asked if he could pop one—it would be fun, in a grotty way—but she'd gone crying to their mother who took Timmy into his room for "a talk." He was never too keen on those little chats. Afterward he made a point of jumping up and down on his bed to shake off the cloud of seriousness in the room.

Zit Queen—he'd heard an older boy describe a girl at school that way, and Timmy liked the sound of it—had gone to the washroom when they first arrived. Timmy wondered what girls could possibly do in the bathroom for the hours and hours they logged in there.

He has set up an ingenious dirt-bike race on Gramps's rug, with pillows and the bolster off Gramps's bed as hills, and Gramps's cane as a fence on the straightaway; he is concentrating on which of his riders is going to win. One of the dirt bikes has spun out of control already and gone skidding off under the bed. Timmy crouches lower to peek under the spread, a quilted floral thing that hangs almost to the floor; he isn't entirely sure he wants to crawl underneath there to retrieve it. Elsewhere in the house are some odd smells, coming off the old people themselves, their wheelchairs and clothing. The rug in Gramps's room gives off an unidentifiable odour up close. Tim slides his arm under the bed as far as he can reach. Nothing. He lifts the spread and peers again. There it is, way over on the other side, almost against the wall. He puts his arm under again and then his head and some of the other shoulder, squirming on his belly to reach the plastic figure. He hears his mother leave the room. When she returns he is back at his tire-squealing, engine-revving race. She bends to him and whispers, "Courtney and I just have to go out for a bit."

"Why?"

"To get some pads," she says.

"There's paper here," says Timmy.

"Not that kind of pad, honeybun. Courtney just got her period."

As always, two pictures form in Timmy's mind: a black dot hovering cartoon-style over his sister's head and a river of blood gushing from between her legs. That would be awesome but no, there she is in the hallway, looking ordinary. Pouting. He tugs at his mother's skirt.

"You could borrow some from one of the ladies here."

His mother does that thing with her mouth again. "No, honey, but we won't be too long."

Timmy is alone with his grandfather. He roars the motorcycles around and around his pillow hills, the cane fence. From the corner of his eye, he sees something hover into view, a hand, extending in shaky slow motion, reaching for him. Timmy draws away and then relents. *It's only Gramps,* he thinks, shifting back into the range of that awkward bird, its tremulous landing. His grandfather's nails are yellowed and spatulate, the knuckles baggy and springy with hair. Moony's mouth is working, and though he's looking at Timmy, it's as if his gaze is a drill through and beyond Timmy's skull. And suddenly the grip on his shoulder goes from doddering to firm, and the boy is pressed down and then, in a surprisingly swift manoeuver, lifted onto his grandfather's knee. He can smell clean flannel and musty breath. *Old guts,* he thinks, oddly not minding. At least his grandfather doesn't smell like some of those old guys downtown, that pissed-in ashtray smell.

"I loved her so much." There is a long silence, and then, "Best thing that ever happened to me."

Moony raises his hands to his head and winces, as if with a headache. Timmy takes the opportunity to slide off Moony's boney knee, but settles himself close by on the rug, leaning against the chair and occasionally offering his eight-year-old version of the consoling pat, a quick tap-tap on his grandfather's brown loafer. The old hand, shaking once again, comes to rest on the arm of the easy chair.

Timmy's used to Gramps going in and out, like those lights people have on their porch at Christmas. His mother has explained that old people see the past more clearly than the present. So even before Gramps says her name, "Kate," Timmy knows when he's talking about Nana. And now Gramps is off again in that vivid world behind his eyes. *The lake and stars and a moon so bright you could read your watch by it, and Peepo wanted to go out in the canoe with me.* Timmy, only half-listening, sees the moon's path on the water and hopes that he and his dad will go on another camping trip this summer. *I knew Katie knew him,* and they'll catch fish and cook it over the fire. *But he made it sound like more than that,* and they can take that old pan and make popcorn on the coals. *He wouldn't shut up about her,* and get up early in the morning and go out in the canoe and fish again. *And then he asked me, did I know if the kids were mine,* and maybe see a snapping turtle. *I slugged him,* or a horned owl, they've seen them before and sometimes bald eagles too. *We almost went over then,* Dad said maybe late August after the bugs. *I guess he thought I was gonna hit him again, so he did this weird dive over the side.*

Gramps's hand has slipped off the armrest, is dangling now beside Timmy's ear. Which means he's dozing. It's like that buzzy fog Timmy feels some mornings if he's stayed up too late reading comics under the covers with a flashlight. His mother calling him for breakfast is like those announcements over the PA at school, bossy but easy to ignore. It's like his head is surrounded by a velvety cloud and though the voice pulls him toward waking, though the light pulls him by the shoulders, his dream won't let him go.

So, is that half-asleep or half-awake? Timmy squints his eyes, and the room is transformed into watery lozenges of colour and light. They keep the heat on pretty high. Timmy leans his head back against his grandfather's chair.

I'll just close my eyes for a minute.

He is swimming on a broad band of moonlight out into the lake. Far ahead, underwater, is a granite boulder, and rocking on it, back and forth, a crescent of gold. As he swims he encounters small areas where the dark water feels sort of swirly, each vortex someone who has gone ahead into the lake: an older woman in a plain cotton dress with a sad expression on her face, and then a bullish looking man and a dog, and Timmy sees, with that dream vision that will make no sense when he wakes but feels so right and easy now, that on that still distant rock and in the sickle's curve a figure is forming, a beautiful lady with open arms. It's Nana, smiling at him, just like she does from the photo on his dad's dresser, and now, keeping pace at his side, stroking with muscular ease, Moony himself, not Gramps but the younger Moony who died and came just halfway back, pulling ahead, swimming straight and strong, and Timmy slows down and hangs there for a while in the water and the sound of the moon rocking back and forth is of someone calling his name in a voice as loud as light.

White Crow

On hunting trips, Don would sleep in his van for two or three nights. He'd set up his Coleman stove and lamp and erect a bug tent if the mosquitoes were particularly bad. He heated cans of pork and beans; he made up big messes of bacon and eggs. If he had managed to find a moose or a deer kill, in their seasons, he fried the liver with onions and potatoes. By the fourth day he was ready to check into a motel for a shower and someone else's cooking.

He walked into the diner in Wawa with his customary shyness. His hair was freshly washed and combed close to his head. Under his tan windbreaker, a striped shirt, clean if a little wrinkled, except over his ample stomach where the cotton stretched taut. His pants were clean, too. He had shaved, and on his right cheek a tiny piece of toilet paper was glued with a spot of blood.

He had his pick of tables; at just past four in the afternoon, the place was empty. The young waitress wore her uniform over jeans, hair held in a pink clip, pancake make-up to cover acne scars. He ordered a steak. The girl snapped her gum and asked her rote questions.

"Medium rare," he answered. "Ranch."

"Baked, please."

She took the menu and walked toward the kitchen. A minute later, she was back with a basket of rolls and the little peel-off plastic containers that held a dab of butter each. These had obviously just come out of the fridge, maybe even the freezer, because the pats were firm and unyielding beneath the tip of his knife. He was intent on scraping a few curls of butter off one of the frozen lumps and pushing them into the curved side of his bread plate—to soften the butter before spreading it on his roll—when he noticed someone in his peripheral vision.

An older, white-haired woman has just taken a seat at a nearby table. She smiles.

"She forgot to take the butter out."

"Pardon?"

"Of the fridge; she's supposed to do it when she comes on shift at two, but she forgets because she's got that numb-skulled boy on her mind."

Something about the woman feels familiar, comfortable. And not counting the girl, they are the only two in the restaurant.

"The boy in question is my nephew, and he's got that white girl all fired up; she thinks they're gonna get married," She lets out a laugh partway between a cackle and cough.

"What's funny about that?"

She snorts. "He's in love with an older girl on the reserve, but they won't marry, either. Come Christmas that poor boy's gonna get high and drown in his own puke."

There it is: the tingling sensation up his spine. The light in the room is changing.

She leans toward him; wraps a hand around his wrist.

"You're wondering if I'm like you."

He stares at her, at the milky cataract in her one eye, the soft folds of wrinkled brown skin, the slight frown that shifts and becomes a smile. When she lets go of his wrist, his skin feels hot where she's touched it.

"You took the liver."

"You were in the woods?"

"Spent my whole life in the woods, young man."

He almost laughs, "I'm not so young." His one vanity is the bottle of Grecian Formula in his bathroom cabinet.

"Younger than me, son."

"How old are you?" As soon as it's out, he regrets the question. His aunt always told him it was rude to ask women their age.

"We didn't keep track back then, one season passed and another. And then they took us all away to the schools."

"I'm sorry," he says.

"Not your fault," she replies. "But I'd guess 100 or 102."

He raises his eyebrows. She either doesn't notice or doesn't care. He drains his beer.

"Can I buy you one?" he nods toward the now empty bottle.

"I don't drink, but I tell you, what I wouldn't give sometimes for a cup of sweet tea and fry bread. I'd settle for pie, since nobody but my sister Annie and I can make a decent piece of fry bread."

"I'll order a tea for you," he says.

She laughs again, an indulgent cackle, "You can go ahead and try."

His bladder is making him uncomfortable. He stands. "I'll be back."

"Don't worry, I'll see you soon enough."

Her voice has gone soft; for a moment their eyes lock. Her gaze is so tender and accepting he could cry, but instead he swings his head around to locate the sign for the washroom, a man following the years and deep habits of shyness, and stands up from his chair with a hand on his back to straighten the kink there, and in the stiff gait of arthritis, moves between tables, making his way across the restaurant.

When he got back to his table his steak was waiting. He started to eat. Five and then ten minutes passed. He motioned the waitress over.

"Did she leave?"

"Who?"

"At that table," he pointed. "An older lady."

The waitress looked confused.

"White hair," he said. "Native. She was right there chatting with me."

"Nobody's been in besides you."

"But I was talking to her. She was sitting right there," he protested. "Grey hair in braids. She had on a red sweater. Silver feather earrings."

The gum chewing stopped. "I'll get Gus," she said, already walking towards double doors that separated the kitchen from the dining area. In a moment she returned with a wiry fellow in a stained apron, his forehead shiny beneath salt-and-pepper hair.

"Diane says you're looking for someone?"

Don described her.

Gus sighed. "Sounds like Nelly White Crow."

The hairs at the back of Don's neck rose. "White Crow?"

"That was her name."

"Was?"

"She's gone, my friend."

"She left already?"

The cook frowned. "This vale of tears. She *died*—oh, six years back? In her nineties. Used to come in every Sunday for tea and pie. Sat right there."

Don stared at the empty chair then looked back at the cook.

"I'd lay off the suds if I was you." Gus raised his apron and wiped his face then turned and walked back to the kitchen. Diane sucked in her cheeks and followed her boss.

Don stared at his plate. In an unconscious gesture, his finger touched the pool of meaty juices and then his lips. He heard her say it again: *I'll see you soon enough*.

Spend enough time in the woods you see everything. Slapping beavers, a mink sleek as tar over rocks, snakes laid out along tree branches, ravens pecking at the reeking remains of turtles. There was that time the marten chased a rabbit right past his outstretched foot when he stopped to eat his sandwich. Osprey carrying fish in their talons. And strange things, nature's aberrances: the animals with distemper, a red squirrel teetering across his camp site, dragging its back legs. Rodents went through boom and bust cycles. Some summers there'd be so many, you'd see them everywhere, young chipmunks skittering the ramp of a fallen tree and leaping, literally leaping, into the water, forced to swim across wide coves in search of territory, such little creatures paddling so far. He'd seen a gull pluck one right out of the water. On portage trails he'd walk into an odour strong enough to make him grimace, the stink of bears. Skinny wolves. A pair of horned owls giving him the hairy eyeball. A mallard with her lower beak dangling from the hinge of her jaw, not long for the world. Albinism, when normally black animals are spotted with white. Earlier that day, he'd watched that peculiar crow, white against the surrounding conifers, circling over the moose kill. After a minute, the ghostly bird swooped down to peck at a ball joint protruding from the abandoned carcass then circled, rising, singing one rough note before she disappeared into silver sky.

Almost a year had passed since their mother's death. Their father had a new wife but hadn't moved her into the house, nor had he moved the boys into his town apartment. There was a German housekeeper, Anna, who cooked and cleaned. Their father had given her the night off and made scrambled eggs and fried potatoes, a meal the boys loved, but Donny didn't trust the mood of the evening. All week he had walked around the house feeling that he was saying goodbye to it. So when their father cleared his throat and began to speak, only Paul sat with wide wet eyes. Donny stared at his plate and heard what he already knew. The house was to be sold. "You boys need a woman's care," said their father. "Someone who knows you." So it wasn't going to be *her*. She'd come out to the house just the one time; it didn't take her long to make a tour. She was pretty, smartly dressed, and not inclined to smile.

The morning after eggs-for-supper, their father told them to pack their suitcases. He was driving them to Auntie Vi's.

Before getting into the car, Donny called for Scamper. His father laid a hand on his shoulder. "Vi won't have an animal in the house."

"So you'll take him to town?"

"He'll go to the Finns's." This was the older couple on the neighbouring farm.

He had known he would lose Scamper, but he'd had to try.

In the car, Donny asked, "We'll see you Pops, on weekends?" The question hung, plaintive and ominously unanswered, in the contained air. Their father finally spoke, "Listen boys, it's hard for me. There's going to be another mouth to feed."

Beside him, Paul was making chewing motions, like a cow. Donny frowned and cradled an imaginary baby in his arms. Paul looked stricken.

"Your Auntie Vi couldn't have kids. Seems to me you two boys are the answer to her prayers."

Except that Auntie Vi hadn't prayed for two half-grown boys. The first night in her house—it would always be her house, never theirs—Vi made them kneel on the carpet and pray.

"Amen." Vi turned down the sheets of the bed. Paul crawled in, but Donny stayed where he was, looking uncertainly at his aunt and over her shoulder at the door, still open into the hallway.

"What are you waiting for Donny?"

"Both of us?" he asked. "In the same bed?" It wasn't the sharing he minded so much as Paul's bed-wetting. He felt Vi's quick, hard slap on his rump and scooted up onto the soft mattress.

"This isn't the Taj Mahal, Mr. Mucky-muck. Your mother spoiled you."

It wasn't said in a mean way, but Donny could see she'd brook no argument. She turned off the lamp on the dresser. From the doorway, she said, "Get some sleep."

Donny dreams of Paul. In the dream his brother is an adult, but he's driving too fast to stop or even swerve when a jack-knifed truck spills into his lane on the 401. At the instant of impact he loses consciousness and therefore misses the conflagration, the giant ball of fire that is his tumbling car.

The next night at dinner, Donny asked for more mashed potatoes—Vi rose and carried Donny's plate to the stove where she spooned not one but two large spoons of potatoes onto it. She poured gravy over top of that. It was more than he wanted but Donny ate it under his aunt's steady gaze.

Boys, she explained, were naturally more sinful than girls. It was a pity her sister had lost the baby; a little girl would have made "all this," her hand swept a loose spiral over the table, "a more rewarding arrangement. But it was God's will."

Donny said nothing. Vi was wrong. The baby—his full sister, now just eight months old—had lived; he knew this the way he knew things about other people, as a small and isolated certainty untethered to before-and-after or why or how. That is, he knew she was alive but not where she had ended up or who had adopted her or if she was happy. He just hoped she was because she was the continuation—the replacement spirit—for the one person who had loved him unconditionally. The baby of his father and the new wife, the baby his father had referred to obliquely as "another mouth to feed" was not born yet. The fates of his sister and half-sister would remain forever closed to him. Their father would visit less and less frequently over the next few years, eroding out of their life until the only contact was a card with money—ten dollars for birthdays, five dollars for Christmas. Eventually, even those dried up. Don wakes up one morning in his unhappy marital bed knowing *his father has died*. But this inarguable fact does not include the name of the funeral home or even the town, and even if it did he would be disinclined to attend the service of the man who stopped behaving like a father years earlier.

On winter evenings, with the windows closed and the curtains drawn, there was a pall of smoke above the two easy chairs in the sitting room. Donny sometimes snuck a cig or two of his uncle's (never his aunt's; she counted) and smoked behind the barn, hating the taste but closing his eyes when the sensation of dizziness came. It gave him a temporary reprieve; it provided an aura beyond the chores and yoke of necessary gratitude that was his life. It was 1947 and Vi was a barren woman in a rural area. Even if people didn't blame her for this, it set her apart. He remembered stories his mother had told of her own childhood and a fun-loving Violet. Those stories didn't jive with the adult she'd become. Like the other women up and down the farm dirt roads and lanes of southern Ontario, she baked bread on Tuesday, washed sheets on Wednesday, and went to church on Sunday in a small hat with a startled piece of tulle over its brim. But sometimes those women waved to him from their porches; sometimes they smiled at each other in church or tousled the hair on the heads of their children.

Uncle Buck was taciturn. Donny could see the disappointment in his aunt's eyes when she looked at her husband.

They'd run out of butter on Wednesday. Three mornings of dry toast, and their potatoes and peas at supper that night and the next had been "naked," a word that had earned Paul a cuff to the head from his uncle. Perhaps he too was unhappy that his lunchtime sandwiches of ham or well-done beef had, instead of a coating of butter, only a thin slick of Keen's hot mustard. For the boys it was bread and jam or sorghum. Donny, hoping to compensate for the lack of butter, asked if they could have meat "just once?" to which Auntie Vi had managed another lesson in the shape of a single slice of bread each, unwrapped, in their lunch tins on Friday.

That noon hour, alone in their corner of the schoolyard, the two hungry boys nursed their hurt pride and committed a small and self-penalizing act of rebellion. If gluttony was high on Vi's list of wrongs, waste was the ultimate sin. The boys tore and squeezed pieces of the dry and unadulterated bread into small greyish lumps between their fingers and inserted them into the cracks of the cedar rail fencing. On the way home they found and ate windfall apples that made their tummies ache, and Donny offered to do the dishes though it was Paul's turn because he wanted to be alone in the kitchen to stick a spoon into the jam and lick it before dropping the evidence into the soapy water.

Later, two farmers drove dusty trucks into the yard for a game of cards that moved among the three farms on Friday evenings. Perhaps in other houses they were invited inside. At Vi's they stayed on the porch. They ate cherry loaf or banana loaf cut into small rectangles that Donny brought out on a tray. They spiked their cups of strong tea with shots from a mickey tucked under the cushion of the porch swing.

The rest of the weekend Uncle Buck alternated only the most imperative chores with long snoring naps on the couch.

Donny was old enough to remember liking Saturdays. Their mother would make picnics, and she would sit on the shore and call out encouragement while their father played and swam with them in the river.

But with Vi, it was a day to wash windows, change bedding, beat rugs, or any of a dozen tasks. Today's chore? Making butter. At the beginning, he and his younger brother and aunt were taking turns with the paddle, but Donny knew their churning would be for nothing. Flies, attracted to the milky smell, to the sheen of sweat on young necks and forearms, hovered. Their aunt smoked; she said it kept the flies away. He hated the bitter tang on her breath when she leaned around him to clear the table. He leaned toward the stove and the partly congealed bacon fat in the cast iron pan, a smell he liked. She was a stickler about cleanliness with this one exception, the well-seasoned skillet. When no one else was in the kitchen, Donny sometimes wiped a bit of bread across greasy iron.

The breakdown of teamwork occurred with Paul wandering off. Their aunt announced she had to see to the ironing. Donny had now been churning for an hour on his own. It wasn't coming, though he'd already sung his little song fifteen times:

Come butter, come,
Come butter, come,
Peter stands at the gate,
Waiting for a buttercake.
Come butter, come.

Donny sighed.

Paul was Vi's favourite, and she might, with a minimum of grumbling, soon make iced tea or lemonade and take him a glass. Then she'd put her feet up and flap an old whicker fan in front of her face. She'd leave Donny to finish the butter.

He added more ice to the water around the churn, and finally he could feel the resistance against the paddles. After another hour of pressing the moisture out, he had a couple of pounds of pale yellow butter, which he put in one of Vi's big bowls. He was covering it with a clean cloth when she came back into the kitchen.

Donny surprised himself by blurting, "It'll be spoiled."

"What are you talking about?" She glared at him.

"Nothing, it's just," he could feel his cheeks burning, "gonna be spoiled," he repeated lamely.

"You're the spoiled one," said Vi, giving him a little punch in his arm, sore now from so much churning. She pointed to the stairs that lead to the cellar. The coolest part of the house, it was the best place to store the butter. He stood and eased himself around her.

What had made the butter so stubborn was the premonition that had shaped his dream last night. He knew he shouldn't put the big bowl downstairs, but he couldn't explain why and he didn't want Vi to hit him again. Downstairs, he waited until he heard her footsteps above, crossing the kitchen floor and exiting into the hallway. He came up out of the cellar and slipped out the back door. Two hours later he was in the field bringing in the cows when the storm blew in: towers of bottom-heavy cumulus, a blue-black pot lid closing down the sky. The bolt of lightning that hit the house did only the damage Donny had seen in his dream, singing the length of the chimney, hopping from the bricks to the shelf with the butter bowl on it. The bowl exploded, coating everything with singed butter: the walls and dirt floor, Uncle Buck's tools, and endless jars of pickles, jams, and tomato chow-chow. And of course everything had to be wiped once and wiped again. It fell to Donny to do the bulk of this. Aunt Vi had to lie down with a cloth on her head because of the shock and the headache brought on by the change in air pressure.

For days afterward she gave him strange sideways glances, and once he caught her making a hurried sign of the cross.

Donny was seventeen when he first noticed his bride-to-be two pews in front of him at church. Much to Vi's surprise, he suddenly blossomed into an ardent churchgoer. Myrna had large pretty eyes behind her glasses and a small waist. Farm work had made him strong and tanned. He was too young and unaware of his own psychological tendencies to recognize that he was wooing his own long-gone and beloved mother. They had a shy courtship: church teas, walks, and the occasional barn dance.

He finished grade eight and had been helping out full time on the farm until a gravel quarry was proposed in the area. Uncle Buck and Auntie Vi sold for a decent profit and moved into town. Paul moved with them. Donny applied his strength and an aptitude for engine tinkering to a job in Caledon. He waited until he had been working for a year and had enough money to rent an apartment in town before he popped the question. They had their first child and then another. Myrna agitated until they moved to Toronto. They moved into a flat in the west end and both found jobs in the industrial area north of them. Don worked hard, but the larger workplace suited him less than the small town outfit, where he'd taken on many tasks and been respected for his responsible approach and quiet manner. After their youngest was born, they combined their factory wages to make a small down payment on a house on a little side street called Dublin. It had worn siding and a postage stamp front yard by the railroad tracks. By then they had been together seven years, and Don found that he was no longer married to that angelic ghost but to an even more cantankerous version of his Auntie Vi. On occasion, out of quiet desperation, Donny walked to a nearby tavern on a Friday night then swayed or stumbled home and slept it off sloppily on Saturday while Myrna clanged pots and vacuumed outside the bedroom door. And yet they managed in the way of all unhappy families, each in his or her own cloud of depression or distraction and the kids outside or at their friends' homes until bedtime.

At seventeen, Don Jr. was as tall as his father and almost as big with a temper. An argument between them escalated to a shoving match. By the time the fight was over and both of them were leaning, stunned, at either end of the front hall, the bickering and detente that had been family life at number three Dublin Street was over. Myrna came home just as the boy was heading down the front path with a duffel bag. She screamed at Don for an hour and then, in furious silence, packed bags for herself and the girls. She took the car and drove to her parents, two hours north of the city. In August, his daughter Anita returned. She'd caught a bus to the city and walked into the kitchen where her father sat drinking a cup of tea.

"Can't you and Mom make it up?"

He had shrugged. "Neats, you know what she's like ..."

"Can I live with you and go to school here?"

He said nothing. He adored his daughters but had grown shy with Anita when she hit puberty. He would never say, but she was his favourite, having inherited his mother's sunny nature and looks, dark hair in a ponytail. She was lean and athletic, a kid who played on lots of teams, and her ready smile made her popular. It was that optimism that had propelled her into the city, though he suspected she missed her friends more than "life with Dad."

He couldn't go against Myrna, just as he had never been able to stand up to Vi. Even if Anita wouldn't admit it, he understood that his soon to be ex-wife would never let her eldest daughter live with him. She would cite the standard wisdom of the era. Children needed their mothers.

These certainties crossed his mind along with a yearning for the loving family he had known as a young boy. He wanted to tell Anita he loved her, he wanted to say he was proud of her for the gumption he could not raise in himself. No answer rolled off his tongue because too many formed in his mind.

The divorce was uncontested. He gave his wife cash for half of the house and kept up support payments. He drove up for restaurant visits with his daughters every month—Myrna either didn't know or wouldn't tell him where Don Jr. was living—and these slowed down to every other month and then once a season, not because he didn't want to see them but because the girls had their "activities" and were just plain bored with the man across the table in his faded but pressed clothes. If Anita had a basketball practice or a game then Kathy wouldn't come. His fatherly link to his youngest daughter was tenuous at best; she'd only been eight when they left. It was Anita who informed him that Myrna was remarrying. Don remembered Al from elementary school, a brash, fair-haired boy who'd made good. He'd inherited the local hardware business from his father and ran a summer camp as well. Anita graduated from high school with honours and applied to university out of the province. Don took on extra shifts to pay part of her tuition. Kathy married right out of high school, in the same church where he and Myrna had wed; she was her mother's daughter. He was not invited.

By then Don was accustomed to his fate. In his loneliness he maintained that he had made the right decision: children needed their mothers. When the older waitresses at the diner teased him about dating, he muttered that he was"done with all that."

It had started with that steak in Wawa, a lead weight in his belly. He was glad he was in a hotel and not in the van that night because of the sudden onset of emptying diarrhea. He dozed rather than slept, but at two in the morning, then three, then four thirty, spasms in his gut propelled him across the worn carpet to the bathroom. He wished he had a candle to light against the smell. And even on the way back to Toronto the next day, he felt uncertain in his bowels, pulling in at gas stations and using their restrooms, but there was nothing to get rid of, just the peristaltic grip and release, an ass-spit, and the low headache and dry mouth of illness.

He stopped drinking beer. Ginger ale helped with the gas, but still his belly swelled, and the diarrhea was now chronic. He'd dream he'd gotten out of bed and gone to the toilet, but instead he woke in his own mess. The frequency of his accidents finally pushed him to seek medical advice. At a nearby clinic he was glad to be seen by the male doctor from India because the other doctor was a pretty blond. The young man pressed on his belly and ordered tests.

Two weeks later he sat in a blue plastic chair across from the specialist. From the conversation one word became a neon tattoo in the murk and shadow behind his eyes. Cancer.

On the day of his surgery a porter rolled him on a gurney down the hall. The lights overhead were too bright, and he felt a swooping nausea in the elevator. In a room painted robin's egg blue, men and women in surgical masks leaned across him. A clear plastic apparatus was placed over his nose and mouth. The room went dark.

He is flying above a river curling through a shallow depression or swamp, the yellow-green and red-brown furze of bog islands, drowned stumps toward the shore. He sees a cow moose and her calf, a heron flapping low over the spongy land; feels the sun on his back as he rises higher, higher, over trees now, the land below dropping away, an endless stretch of green suddenly subdivided, pitted by grey-brown rectangles, straight-edged in a wonky grid with roads, clusters of buildings, and a water tower like a mushroom. Farther up he enters white fog and then bright lights against which he squeezes his eyes, and the sound of static was now pierced with echoes and buzzers, too-loud voices and the squeaking of rubber soles on linoleum.

The flesh around the stitches felt as if occupied by angry bees, and after a painkiller he got a bit giddy and then fell asleep. Some nights he was his wound, all his concentration pulsing towards that tear in his gut, the pain an insistent drum that beat him down into a black space rent with red light and clanging sound; he wanted to sleep and couldn't until the nurse gave him another pill.

They came and went, black and brown and occasionally white faces, cold or warm hands and latex gloves, deep or harsh or kind voices, efficient women and men who threw open the curtains and tugged at his bedding or rolled him to one side and fiddled with his dressings, poking at his tender belly. The surgeon came, his voice flat in apology, "It seems the cancer …" at that word, Don's ears were filled with a roar of white noise and though the doctor droned on, his voice reminded Donny of the bleating, bawling piglets and lambs he had once had in his care. He remembered their crooked little paths toward the ewe or the sow and the torment of losing one or more to a fox or coyote. Once, he'd witnessed a red-shouldered hawk pluck a barn mouse off the ground and another time a gopher, and just now the white crow had flown to the windowsill and cocked her head in.

"How long have I got?"

The doctor raised both eyebrows and pushed out his lips as if to stall until, Don, with uncharacteristic vehemence said, "It's *my* life."

"I'd say it's a matter of weeks."

After the doctor left Don closed his eyes, but his mind was a restless bird, flying and alighting on branches and fences. He was thinking of blueberry pie and his slippers waiting by the back door, and of his two or three favourite camping spots, and the worn patches on the arms of the sofa in his aunt's living room, and what was the name of those flowers that came up each spring along his neighbour's walkway, mauve and yellow? He wasn't going to look down on them again, so brave and surprising against the dry sticks of last year's plants.

He'd known that he was dying since that day in the Wawa diner. Since she'd turned to him and lifted the corners of her old mouth in a young smile of welcome and sorrow.

When he could walk down the hospital halls unaided, he was discharged. One afternoon, he answered his front door and there stood Anita, slim and older now, better looking than anyone might have imagined coming from him, in her smart suit and pumps. He got less than a year but more than the hedged bets offered by the doctor, enough for a few family visits, "Daddy, these are your grandkids," and if it didn't beat all, his ex-wife was there, now a widow, looking smaller and just as tired as he was; their daughter was running the show, a nice roast chicken and potatoes, not that he could eat much, but he obliged with a few bites of the cake, and the camera was popping away.

These photos will be at my funeral.

Not an open coffin but an urn on display with the recent family photos and older ones of him with a strung-up deer carcass and a medium-sized trout held shoulder high. His granddaughter read a poem; his daughter read the Twenty-third Psalm; the funeral director did his bit and it was over.

Don Jr. offered to take the ashes up north and scatter them, but he only got as far as his small low-rise apartment in downtown Sault St Marie. "Course I done it," he lied to his sister when she called. After a long drag on his cigarette, he embellished: "Over by Espanola, place he took me once."

There had been fishing trips in his boyhood, baked beans and wieners, marshmallows on sticks at night, and sometimes a moon so bright they could play cards seated on rocks by the side of the lake. But by thirteen, Don Jr. had tired of the quiet rhythm of weekends in the bush with his dad. On their last one together, he had snuck two cans of his father's beer and smoked a joint in the woods behind their tent. The next day he slept till noon. After that trip Don Jr. simply said no to every suggested camping trip until his father stopped asking.

Not that he didn't hunt and fish now. In fact he craved it after a week at the mill. But he never admitted this to his dad because he hadn't spoken to him since the fight that propelled him out of the house a week after his seventeenth birthday. He was making up for it now, talking alone and aloud in his living room, nightly orations, odes to the steel urn perched on a shelf, all the things unsaid but now voiced in belligerence as beer was replaced by rye and the bottom of the bottle appeared.

His sisters and mother had found happiness or at least something that resembled peace, but Don Jr. had not. He didn't know why his anger propelled him to pick fights in bars or why his one attempt at a relationship had ended with a restraining order because he'd burned down a shed on his girlfriend's property. She'd had a six-year-old boy that Donny had grown to love. It was the loss of the boy more than the woman that he regretted. He'd spent short stints in jail for public drunkenness and brawling, and all of it was his father's fault. Because it *was*.

In a fit of rye-stoked anger he crossed the room, grabbed the urn and strode down the hall with it to the garbage chute. No sooner done than regretted, and so he stumbled down to the basement, rooted through the reeking bin at the bottom of the chute and came up with the now sullied container, and swooped it up under his arm like a misbehaving toddler. He headed back upstairs, and as he climbed towards his apartment on the fourth floor he was rising up through inchoate memories, the legacy of petty regrets and their resulting regrettable decisions—his life!—the passing of inadequacy from father to son to son, generations of it, congealed in a middle-aged man pulling open a stubborn door.

He placed the urn unsteadily on the shelf.

He has woken early—the habit of a lifetime. He fishes a mug from the kitchen sink and rinses it with tap water, then fills it from the kettle and adds a heaping teaspoon of instant coffee. A small drop bounces free of the cup's rim and scalds his hand, eliciting the one expletive, "Fuck!" but the tiny mark it makes is soon forgotten with more of that rhythmic, indeed meditative, stirring in of Carnation milk. He walks out of the standing-room-only kitchenette and into the living room, where he stares out the window at sky framed to one side by a tall black spruce. His low-rise apartment building sits on a hill. Beyond a series of flat and peaked roofs are more trees, the lush broccoli of maple, oaks, and fluttering aspens, and beyond these the spindly tips of more spruce. Above them all and moving northwest with a certain perky enthusiasm are three baby cumulus. A southern system will envelop the town in day or two.

But for now the day is promising warmth, pleasant breezes, good fishing weather, and he has sidelined the worst of his hangover, for the moment, with that quotidian combination of caffeine, sugar, and nicotine.

He puts the urn in a plastic grocery bag and carries it down to his truck, drives into town, and parks on the main drag. He enters the greasy spoon he has frequented for years. The waitresses know his order, and today he is efficient rather than chatty, grunting as the coffee is poured and dumping the correct amount on the counter by the cash after he has polished off two eggs over-easy, sausages, hash browns, and unbuttered whole wheat toast. He drives out of town a few kilometres and down a lane familiar to locals, leaving the motor running while he gets out to open the wire and steel gate. In short order he has parked inside the fenced property, retrieved the grocery bag and its square contents from the passenger seat, unlocked the metal box behind the cab of the truck, removed a long, zippered vinyl bag and locked the box again. He walks through piles of separated refuse: wood, metal, rubber, and plastic, a large mound each. Breathing more shallowly, he passes composting household garbage, scattering the scavenging birds until he is at the far end of the dump. There is a stretch of old cedar fence here. He places the urn on the top rail, but it won't stay. He casts his eye behind him at the various piles until he sees two old crates, which he stacks, one above the other against the fence. The construction is a bit rickety, so he grabs a tire, wedges the lower crate into it, and twists two lengths of wire between the crates. Atop this makeshift tower he places the urn. A brief glance at his watch shows that it is almost noon.

The urn is now resting at chest height. He slams a few cartridges into the rifle he has unzipped from its bag. With his back to the urn, he measures out twenty paces. Turns, takes aim *right through the heart*. Fires. After half a second of ringing silence, the gulls behind him scream and wheel up. The ravens are vocal and on the fly now, heading over the trees. He watches them go. A single smallish gull that has taken flight with the black birds turns and circles back toward the dump. The shot has bounced the urn over the fence and into the bushes, and as if to mock him, the white bird pulses above the stacked crates and alights, pulling its small wings into its body, walking in delicate circles around the crate end.

This is a man in no mood to be mocked by a stupid gull. He shoulders his rifle, and as he sights down the barrel he sees that it is not a gull at all but a white crow.

"Fucking freak," he whispers as he squeezes the trigger.

HYPOTHERMIA

It took a certain personality to work in the camps, nothing but bush and the occasional helicopter drop-off. No tv, no movies. There was always a generator that ran the radio, and they'd listen to CBC and the northern station in the evening. Books, cards, skiing, and snowshoeing. It took stability and self-reliance. Kathryn had been in camps where someone couldn't cut it. It was rough on everyone.

Up at six, big breakfast, check the radio for the day's weather, not that the predictions were always all that accurate: northern storms were mercurial. "Wind like a woman," Randy would say. Then out in the bush working the lines, doing what needed to be done. Daylight was a precious resource in the winter months, so lunch was eaten on the trail. Packed by the men from whatever she—the cook and only woman on site—laid out. Then more work until four thirty, five, and back to camp for dinner. At that hour the men were ravenous; it was amazing what they could put away: meat and potatoes and veg and desserts, at least two helpings of each. And by that time maybe a game of cards or cribbage, a bit of reading, a bedtime snack and bye-bye, you were kissing your pillow.

When it was really cold and clear they might see the northern lights. It was close to tundra so the trees were short, maybe twice the height of a man, and spread out. Mostly spruce, poplar, aspen. To some people it seemed barren, but she found it beautiful—land to be quiet in. Marten, lynx, and ptarmigan, sitting in the snow or hopping about, birds so white it was hard to notice them unless they were flying away, then you'd see the two black flashes on their tail. The winter days were short, but light seemed to travel far; you felt like you could see a pebble on a hillside miles away.

She liked to be strong, and so she timed her cooking and baking to allow for a couple of hours of exercise: skiing or snowshoeing. She had suffered hypothermia once before, a fact she had downplayed on her application. If you'd suffered it once, you were more susceptible. But she was careful, sticking to known trails and limiting after-dinner walks so that the main tent cabin remained in sight. At night, it gave off a ghostly glow.

The crew had been together for a year, with various leaves and absences. They'd closed up camp for part of the summer and now they were returning. Kathryn and Randy flew in a day ahead with all the food. They ferried snow machines out to the helipad. In the morning, she skied out to greet the helicopter when it arrived. Out of combined shyness and attraction she saved Darrel's hug for last. Was it her imagination or did he hold on longer than the others?

He surprised her one afternoon in the mess tent, a tap on the shoulder while she mixed something in a bowl. When she turned he took a strand of hair and curled it behind her ear.

"Oh," she could feel her cheeks growing warm.

"You're beautiful," he said.

"You're married," she arched her eyebrow and turned back to her cake batter.

"That's over," he said on his way out the door.

They were seated next to one another that evening at dinner: knees pressed, glances sent, caught, and held. After the dishes were done, she went for her customary walk. Minutes later she heard the crunch and grip of boot soles on the packed snow of the trail.

She didn't trust herself to speak. Instead, she pointed overhead where the stars were partially obscured by pulsing veils of green and white. If the sky was electrified so was she; beneath layers of down and wool her skin tingled. She wanted to lean against him, to close her eyes and raise her face to his. Instead she spoke.

"C'mon, I'll race you back."

The next day he rode into camp an hour before the others were due to return. They sat at a small table in the kitchen, drinking tea and talking. After an hour, she rose with reluctance.

"I have to finish dinner," she said.

He stood and pulled her into a hug, planting a kiss in her hair. She stepped back, with her palm against his chest. "Go," she whispered. He raised her hand and pressed his lips to her fingers before he turned and left.

They met that way for three—five ? Ten days?—until the afternoon he pulled her to him and kissed her hard.

"Your cabin," he said, because as the only woman, she didn't have to share.

They were both a little nervous; it was fumbling, funny, and endearing.

Within a week she joked that she was going to start timing her bread around their lovemaking. Talking with him was the easiest thing she'd ever done. Thus the afternoon hours evaporated, both of them scrambling into clothes when they heard a snow machine in the distance.

One day he came to her bed with a sheepish smile. "I've run out of condoms."

From that point on they did what she, smiling, referred to as "other things" including coitus interruptus. They finagled and outright lied to get the same two days off. Kathryn had a furlough owed to her. Darrel invented a family emergency.

The helicopter ride was exquisite torture because they couldn't touch. In town, they pretended to go their separate ways. For two precious days and nights they barely got out of the motel bed except to get into the bath together or for one of them to collect take-out at a local restaurant. They slept in odd cycles, a few hours here and there, and when one or the other woke they sought out the still-sleeping partner's warmth and musk, and by the end of the two days, she'd lost count of how many times they'd come together.

Waiting for the helicopter at the end of that loving and illicit weekend, she had turned to him, "I don't think we can do this."

"What we're already doing?" Briefly, he leaned his shoulder against hers.

"You're still married."

In the course of the weekend, he had admitted that he and Jan were still living together.

"It's over."

"But you haven't told her or …"

"Or what?"

"Or officially separated or been to a lawyer or had the fights. You have ten years of deep habit. When you go home, well …"

"Kath, you gotta let me take care of that."

She buried her face in her hands briefly then took a deep breath and continued: "My last boyfriend was a very good man. Kind. Funny. But we didn't have this," she waved her hand back and forth between them. He caught and squeezed it.

"I'm not finished," she said.

"Okay."

"You and me. It's a rare situation. Maybe you are falling out of love with Jan."

"Fallen. Done."

"And you're restless and I'm …" The ache of tears behind her eyes made her stop.

"Beautiful," he said. "Lovely. Sexy."

She took a deep breath. "I can picture your wife. She's pretty and slim," she pressed her hand to her belly. "Do you know what the gym teacher called me in high school? A *big* girl. Darrel, this," she jerked her thumb towards herself, "is not beautiful. This is what's available."

"Kathryn!"

"I'm the only woman at the camp, the only woman within two hundred miles of our little enclave of tents and seismic equipment. Up here, I represent the entire gender."

"I could have found a she-bear."

"They're hibernating, and don't tease me."

"You're the one I want to be with."

"Yes, *now*, but what about when we're back in the land of slim, sexy women, and I'm looking like the "before" picture in the Weight Watchers ads."

She turned her head so she wouldn't have to read his expression. *Don't beg,* her girlfriends would say. *Don't parade your insecurities in front of him.* Their flight was called.

At the outset, before even that first kiss, he'd said he was separated. Maybe he'd said we're separa*ting*, or it had been more ambiguous, "I left my wife," which could have meant temporarily or "to fly up north." It might not have meant what she wanted to hear: I am a free man and I choose you. Whatever the statement, it had worked. And now she was in over her head and too many of the possible outcomes were painful and unclear.

The need in her, to talk, to wail "what do I do?" was almost unbearable. She yearned for Patty and Judy, girlfriends since junior high. What would they say? Drink with *us*, cry with *us*, but let *him* take the initiative. Men had to stew or distill the emotional thing or put it under mental lock and key while they did something busy and physical and absorbing. Then, they might come to you. Or they would stay away and at that juncture you'd realize they'd seen you as a "friend," someone to confide in, someone who'd cook them a nice meal and give their shoulders a rub. If the woman of their dreams wasn't appearing on the horizon, they'd take sex if it was offered. But they wouldn't find you mysterious and sexy, not like the pretty, skinny, frosty types. On all three fronts she'd have to say "pass," though Darrel had called her "beautiful" thirteen times.

I'm not sure it counts, though, she'd say to Patti and Judy. *Since it was immediately before or after sex.*

Ah, they'd say.

Hanging wet socks beside the stove or punching down dough, putting out a platter of sausages or mixing a batch of cookies, the recollections assailed her. She'd *felt* beautiful in that motel room, walking to the bathroom naked, coming back from a shower and dropping the towel at the edge of the bed, his eyes on her body as she lifted the sheets to reenter the dark swoon of their union, the glorious suspension of time and the outside world. But now at night, alone in her little cabin, when their bodies were no longer pressed hip to hip and breasts to back or chest, and his hand was not cupping her ass and pulling her to him, the words he'd uttered came back to her.

He was still living with Jan.

He was married.

They were cheating on another woman. She'd vowed she never would.

All she could do was give him the space to decide.

At mealtimes, she avoided sitting beside or across from him. She returned to her exercise routines. Days passed. She was skiing one afternoon and heard his snow machine plying the trails. When he found her he turned off the engine and removed his dark glasses.

"Will you take off your skis?" he asked. "Please?"

He might as well have said "take off your clothes" for the way warmth rose up from her knees and the bottom of her stomach fell away. As she stepped out of her bindings, he slid back on the seat and hauled her onto the snow machine, facing him.

She tucked her head so he couldn't kiss her.

"Darrel, I'm confused."

But he nuzzled her neck and began to undo the zips and flaps of outer layers.

When his hand slipped under her shirt she lifted her lips to his.

"You're lucky I wore my brother's long johns," she said.

He grinned, "With their convenient aperture."

Moments later as she straddled him, "You know you're a Canadian …"

"When you screw on a skidoo."

"I think it's 'in a canoe'."

"Something," he said, snuggling his chin into her neck, "for our bucket list."

He talked to her then, holding her to him on the vinyl seat. He had some time off coming up. He was heading to Saskatoon to "face the music."

"That's the end of it," he said. "I promise."

They held each other a while longer. It was she who pulled away first. There was still a coleslaw to be assembled and the long table to be set and all the minutes and hours and days to get through before his departure and more hours and days before his return. When she looked up from clicking her boots into their bindings, he was watching her with such tenderness it took her breath away. She almost said it then. But he donned his sunglasses and drove away with a wave.

She stared after him for a long while, until the cold propelled her into action, poles punching rhythmically beside the lonely shushing of her skis.

A few days later, she announced at breakfast that she would walk lunch out to the guys. Not Jake and Matt, the "pups"—they still told fart jokes, for heaven's sake—but to Randy and Pete. She had an easy dinner in mind, something she could throw together when she got back to camp. It had been glorious the day before, but she'd only managed a half-assed ski on stodgy snow. By mid-morning the sun was high, the sky a perfect blue, and it was mild enough to go gloveless and hatless.

They were all a bit high on the weather.

She saw Darrel just before she left camp. She was wearing ski pants and gaiters over her hiking boots because of the slush, a sweater, and a down vest. He told her she wasn't dressed for the weather, she should go back and put on her bikini. She executed a little jive wiggle with her hand up and her hip out.

"You wish."

They exchanged smiles and then were both suddenly serious, and in his eyes was that look again. *Is that goodbye? Will you keep your promise? I haven't said I love you, but I do. I love you. Do what you need to do. I love you. I'll always love you.* But she knew better than to say any of it. His visit home could change everything.

It would take her a couple of hours to walk out to the coordinates Pete and Randy had given her. She wanted that, time on her own under that singing blue and cloudless sky. In these past few weeks her feelings and moods had been so … *volatile*. Certainty, doubt, exhilaration, anxiety, certainty, doubt …

When she caught sight of the two men, they were bending and squatting, fussing with the equipment. It was one of her private pleasures, to perch on a hill and watch the crews, the men like animated dolls under orange hard hats. On colder days they looked like gummy bears against the snow, puffy bright parkas and white gumbo boots. Today both men were working in shirt sleeves.

She'd brought soup in a thermos and sandwiches and banana bread.

After lunch Pete got on one of the snow machines. He was just turning it around when he hit a slick patch, lost control, skidded off the trail, and stalled immediately. It was a dicey machine anyway; they'd had problems with it for about a month. Pete tried the engine again, but it was screwed. As he swung his leg up and over to get off, his other ankle folded under him, an old football injury.

Randy helped her make a rough splint from a couple of saplings. With Pete's leg the way it was, they couldn't ride three to the seat on the one functional machine. They'd get back to camp and radio for a helicopter. Pete needed to get to the clinic.

Kathryn said, "It's fine. I don't mind going back on my own."

Randy offered to take the pack so she wouldn't have to carry it.

Once they were back in camp, Randy would radio Darrell. "That fucking machine." He'd tell Darrell the coordinates. "Radio me if you can get it started. I'll send Matt and Jake."

"Randy, I know the drill." She could imagine Darrell being a bit testy. He'd warned Randy repeatedly about the troublesome engine. They were too isolated and the weather was too fickle to be dealing with unreliable transportation. Kathryn had echoed the concern. Once. As the only woman in camp, she couldn't appear to nag.

She listened until the dissipation of the engine sound was replaced by the drip and creak of sun-warmed snow and ice. The ground was laced with slanting blue shadows—it made the walking hypnotic. At each juncture where their snow machines had woven new paths across the one she walked, she thought: I'm at a crossroads. We both are.

The pups are waiting in the mess tent, two strapping and perpetually hungry young men. Darrell walks through the door about a minute before Randy.

Matt asks, "When's dinner?"

The four men look at each other.

Randy turns to Darrell, "You didn't bring her in?"

"Wasn't she with you?"

"Fuck," says Randy. "I thought you'd pick her up on the trail."

The light rain of ten minutes ago has increased to sheets of rain. The drumming on the roof is almost deafening.

"Man," says Jake, "it's really coming down."

Now they are all in motion, pulling on rain gear, stuffing Kathryn's into a drybag. Darrel pulls her sweater, scarf, and mitts off a hook and thrusts them at the pups as they push out the door. They'll travel all the spurs to the north of the main trail, the one she took this morning though Darrel's been along it already. But he must have missed her, maybe she took a side route or ventured off through the trees. Maybe she was hiding from him? Oh God. He follows them out, shouts instructions through the wall of rain. The pups share a snow machine. When Darrel goes back into the main cabin, Randy is trying to rouse another helicopter, but it's getting dark, the temperature is plummeting. The dispatcher is firm; he can't risk sending a pilot into freezing rain.

The two men exchange a look.

"One of us stays," says Darrel.

"Okay," says Randy rising from his chair.

"No, I'll go!" Outside, Darrell throws his leg over the machine, twisting the key in the ignition, grateful for the cold rain on his face, slapping back the tears.

He senses the other snow machine travelling the smaller avenues, the two vehicles plying their way in purposeful panic, a moving warp to the haunted empty weft of the main trail. And finally, when they can't see a foot in front of their faces they have to go back. But Darrel can't stop himself from going out under the icy rain every fifteen minutes or so with a pot and a spoon, banging it, crazy now not with fear but the certainty that what he loves is already gone.

The pups manage catnaps after scrounging a makeshift dinner: sandwiches and cocoa. Neither of the older men eat or sleep. Before light they refuel and this time they all go: Darrel, Matt, each on a machine, Jake and Randy sharing another. They are skidding around corners on a massive ice rink that extends as far as they can see. As the sun rises, each tree, each branch, twig, and needle is aureoled in gold.

In the early hours of the morning he wakes with a start, shivering. He has been dreaming of the seismic camp again. Sleep, he knows, will not return. Though it would be wiser to get up, make a pot of coffee, read or see what offerings there are at this hour on TV—potentially a seedy talk show or an old black and white movie—he stays in bed, pulling the comforter up over his shoulders, hugging the pillow beside him the way he hugged Jan in the early years of their marriage, and Kathryn whenever he could.

He had returned, shut down and silent, to Saskatoon; he knew he would never go north again. Jan accused him of having another woman. He felt he owed his wife an explanation but he couldn't betray Kathryn's memory. There were months of détente, depression. He couldn't explain. Jan had a dinner party and served up his loss in the form of an ice sculpture in the centre of the table. The day after the party he delivered a coup de grace to his marriage. There was a certain subliminal equation to it: Jan's symbolic centrepiece and the simple surgical procedure he underwent. It landed him on the couch gingerly holding a bag of ice to his swollen scrotum. In truth, he'd had the appointment booked for weeks.

It was an act of atonement. It was blind justice arising from blind love. Not his wife's guess but his own.

He could still hear the last thing Kathryn said to him.

"You wish."

Yes, he wished. He would go on wishing, that the weather hadn't turned so suddenly, that he'd been in camp when Randy and Pete returned instead of riding out on the trail to join the pups when his walkie-talkie crackled to life. It was Randy asking him to check on the snow machine. He hadn't asked about Kathryn, and Randy hadn't offered. Darrell headed cross-country to the disabled machine. He was preoccupied with the task ahead of him, not the literal task of fixing the snow machine but the psychological heaviness that awaited him in Saskatoon. Disassembling a marriage. And then while he swore and tinkered with the fucked-up engine, the cracked ski and the skewed tracks, the weather shifted. He kept a tarp stowed under his seat; he threw this over the broken machine and left it to the elements, driving back in a suddenly advanced and brooding dusk. He knew he was in a pissy mood: he was giving up a lot for Kathryn but of late she'd been so distant. And wasn't there a small part of him that planned to ignore *her* at dinner, to match her new reserve with his own?

He will never forgive himself this small betrayal.

There were paths everywhere. Too many damned tracks. Although the way they found her, at the end, she was close to camp and halfway up the bank of a creek; it was clear she'd gone through the ice, floundered, then hauled herself out of the water—by this time her hands and feet were probably completely numb. She would have struggled and slipped her way up the slope, and maybe she lost ground and maybe she put her head down for a minute and simply lost consciousness.

The storm blew in a half day earlier than expected. She had not passed

Darrel on the trail because at the creek juncture she had turned; she had in fact taken the wrong turn. She was daydreaming; she was in a hormonal fog; she was starting to get cold.

Four devastated men, the two younger ones with hot tears flowing down their faces, stood in a half circle over the woman that each, in his own way, loved. Her hair had gotten wet because she had no hat. It was frozen in a kind of crazy arc around her head. The sun hit the slope of the creek, and the icy casing that held her to the ground caught its weak rays, and for the last time, Kathryn was beautiful.

She is ambling back to camp along trails punched down by snow machines, trails that cross and double-cross in *Xs* and *Ys* and long lazy loops. Her focus is inward; she has eaten just a little lunch because she is still unsure of her tummy. This morning's breakfast, yesterday's breakfast, and breakfast the day before have all risen the way they came. She is in a protein-deprived reverie: if he comes back from Saskatoon and still wants her, she'll say yes. But for now she has to play out a little line, give him a chance to stand down from what might just be a big, but temporary, need. She is filled with hope and shining with her own clarity, and she doesn't notice that the sky overhead has taken on the consistency and colour of pea soup. She rests a hand on her abdomen, under the layers of vest, sweater, and t-shirt. A month, if that, which makes it what—the size of a peanut?

She is smiling, and when she speaks, just a few words, to the tiny curl of matter sheltered by muscle which itself is cradled by womanly flesh, her voice is low and resonant. It is absorbed by the rough scrubby bark of stunted black spruce. A flock of juvenile ravens flies by overhead, searching for a roost on what would prove the longest of nights. Their ragged call pulls her attention skyward.

From the Beaver God

Eddie Pilcher's wife was in the kitchen at the time of the call. From the way her husband was speaking into the phone, she recognized it as a "house-call." Eddie and his brothers did a brisk trade in the summer, doing small and large fix-it jobs on cottages and boathouses in the area. Coming into fall they offered a package deal to cottagers which involved draining pipes and then taking a boo around the property once a week, shovelling snow off dormers and roofs, checking for deer-damage to fences and, if so, to yards and trees, and keeping an eye out for any leaking or flooding during spring thaw. If anything needed fixing inside or out, the Pilcher brothers were the men to call.

Something about Eddie's manner drew Mary's attention as she brought a bowl of mashed bananas to the table. He was saying "yes" and "no problem," like he always did, but raising his eyebrows at her as she spooned fruit into the baby's mouth. She creased her forehead in reply, creating what Eddie liked to call her Hawaiian frown. First the right then the left eyebrow dipped, and then the right and left again—a continuous figure eight, a manoeuver which Eddie, in the beginning of their relationship, had tried to duplicate in the bathroom mirror. But the more he tried, the more he resembled a spastic chimpanzee, so he left the facial contortions to his wife and then, as now, marvelled at the strange ways of the world.

"Right, then," he said. "I'll come by to get the key." He hung up. "Can you believe it, Mare? That was that woman near Battersea."

"What woman?"

"The tree hugger." Then as an afterthought, he added: "The *ball-buster*."

"Eddie," Mary frowned and cocked her head toward the baby.

"Mary, he doesn't even say 'Dada,' yet. Come on, Sammy," he leaned over the table and kissed his son's nose, "say ball-buster."

"Ba," said Sammy, raising pudgy arms to be picked up.

"You wretch," Mary said. But she was laughing as she pulled the baby out of his highchair. "Take him outside, *buster*. You can play 'ba.'"

On his way through the screened-in porch, Eddie grabbed a small quilt and a plastic ball. Sammy could sit up without help now, his little butt ensconced in a bulky diaper. Eddie walked across his well-kept lawn to the pear tree and lowered his son to the ground. This way Sammy could be in the shade, and Eddie, who sat spread-eagled on the grass, could enjoy the sun. He rolled the ball across the quilt. Sammy's arms bounced up and down, and occasionally one of his pudgy little fists hit but failed to shift the ball except sideways, so Eddie leaned forward and tapped the ball back toward his own legs then picked it up and spun it on his finger. As long as the ball kept moving, his son would be content and Eddie free to ponder.

Among themselves, the Pilcher brothers told disparaging anecdotes about businessmen in golf shirts and thick leather sandals who couldn't caulk a window or clean out an eavestrough. It was easier doing the work for their wives when the men were down in the city, although these days, as many women as men choked the highways on Friday afternoons, talking on cell-phones and looking harassed. There were the urban types: falsely chummy barristers and bankers who chatted with him—about hockey or hunting, as if those were the only subjects on which he might possibly be conversant—over cold beers they offered in the driveway or on the dock. He often lied that he had to get home to take his wife somewhere, not because he didn't want the beer—even though it was a micro-brewery or something *European*—but because he didn't like drinking quickly, standing around near his truck. If the guy didn't have the decency to invite him to sit down or come inside, he didn't want his beer-charity.

Less obnoxious were the ones who did most of their own handiwork but called when they needed specific help, say, with a dead tree leaning over a roof or a rotting dock. Those guys knew that Eddie knew something they didn't, and if they tended to hover while he was doing it, they did it to learn. These were the guys the Pilchers called do-it-yourselfers or DIYs, a group that bothered Eddie less than it did his brothers. Maybe it lowered the percentage of repeat clients, but it tended to raise the incidence of word of mouth. A healthy business, Eddie argued, was built on relationships. Besides, he liked explaining what he was doing. Eddie always thought that if he hadn't gone into the family trade, he would've become a teacher.

Hardest to work with were the people who thought they knew the outdoors better than he did. Tree-huggers had managed to get the spring bear hunt cancelled, and bears were camping out at every garbage dump in the province. Some were forcing their way into houses that bordered Crown land. The Ministry of Natural Resources was spending a lot of money and manpower tracking and shooting nuisance bears. Sometimes Eddie and his brothers joked that the MNR oughta shoot a few nuisance *citizens* while they were at it.

Though he routinely worked for people he didn't exactly respect, he was careful to keep his comments within the confines of family. It was very unusual for Eddie Pilcher to lose his cool with a customer. It was rarer still for Eddie Pilcher to lose his cool with a woman. Which is why he'd almost fallen off his chair when Jill Matthews called. Even as he'd called her "the ball-buster" to Mary, it was more out of shock than any residual animosity.

The Pilchers made courtesy calls—good for business—to new occupants of properties where they'd worked in the past. Eddie had gone by one such house in the fall, introduced himself to the owner and explained his concern: spring thaw and a nearby beaver dam were sure to cause problems in her lower laneway. The conversation ended badly. The winter that followed this exchange was long with plenty of snow. Shorelines were waterlogged the following spring. Eddie wasn't surprised when she finally called. He wore a withering air of "I told you so," while draining her flooded driveway and charged her $400 for what he knew was a $200 job. Now he felt sheepish. He was even a little nervous about going to get the key.

Sammy was popping spit balloons and drooling. A leaf from the pear tree detached and floated down, landing in brown-blond curls. Sammy's chin rose and both arms came up, the two movements enough to topple him over backward. With his legs in the air he chortled; Eddie grinned and swept his son up in his arms.

Mary was right; he should curb the nicknaming tendency. He'd just never expected to hear from Jill Matthews again.

Back in the house, Eddie kicked off his shoes and padded down the hall to the kitchen carrying Sammy. Mary was just finishing the dishes. He'd always liked watching her: the way she narrowed her eyes when she was thinking or chewed the inside of her mouth when she'd misplaced something—the baby's sunhat or a can of soup she swore she'd just taken out of the cupboard. Hard working, like all the Pilcher wives; Mary also had a dreamy side. Even now, after ten years of marriage and three kids, his wife's private thoughts remained a mystery to him. Oh, they talked about all kinds of stuff; every day Eddie came home and told Mary about his day, and every day she filled him in on hers and the kids' and any change or development on their property, crocuses in bloom or hens laying in the cab of the old truck or something funny that had happened to so-and-so down their road. But Mary, like his mother, was—how would he put it—emotionally contained. There was a part of herself she kept private. Sometimes he came upon her on the screened-in porch or in the upstairs hall, and she'd be standing there, a screwdriver or toy in her hand, just staring into space. It was like she'd caught a scent of something on the breeze or gotten distracted by a sound, a couple of crows gossiping in the maple outside, or maybe it was a conversation that had happened long ago that she was hearing, again, in her mind. At those times Eddie might quietly turn and leave her to it, or else he'd come up behind her and tuck his chin into her neck and tease her for being "away with the fairies." It was a phrase he'd heard a lot as a kid. According to the senior Mrs. Pilcher, Eddie had been a dreamy boy.

Mary bent to open the dishwasher. Steam rose and she took a swipe at her face. The baby gurgled and Eddie walked over to his wife.

"Sammy sandwich," he said as he hugged his wife from behind with his one free arm. She made a little appreciative noise in her throat and he released her. She turned and reached for Sammy, nuzzling her face into Sammy's neck.

"I'll be back around two or so. That give you enough time to get to your appointment?"

"I might head in earlier, if Meghan and Jenny get back from the Rosses." Meghan, aged fourteen, had a summer job babysitting the neighbours' children. Jenny sometimes went along and helped.

"Then I'll see you at dinner, honey," Eddie said. Mary gave him a quick smile then pulled up Sammy's shirt and blew a raspberry on her son's tummy. Eddie could hear their giggling all the way out to his shed.

His hip-waders were hanging on a hook by the door. He rolled them into a loose ball and shut the shed door, then walked to his truck and threw the waders in the back. Water levels on some of the small lakes in the region were way up. A worried homeowner at the eastern end of Inverary Lake had called a few days ago, and Eddie and Dwight had driven over to check it out.

There were three houses in a row with sloping lawns down to the lake. To the east was a section of Crown land, heavily treed, but these properties had been cleared decades ago for farmland and later sold into lots and levelled to accommodate houses. Neither Dwight nor Eddie would have bought a place that pretty much screamed flooding, but as they walked the waterfront they kept this opinion to themselves. They poked at the eroded mud bank and explained the options.

"You could try reinforcing with rock baskets," said Eddie.

"Or railway ties," added Dwight.

"I don't get it," the homeowner said. "We haven't had that much rain."

"Oh, it isn't rain," Dwight replied. "It's beavers."

"Beavers?" asked the guy.

"That's right," said Eddie.

They were all silent for a moment, looking out over the wind-ruffled lake.

"Can you do something about that?" the guy asked.

"Hmm," said Eddie.

"I'll pay you, of course."

"No problem," said Dwight.

So yesterday, Eddie hitched his boat trailer to his truck and picked up Brian because Dwight was checking out wind damage to a farmer's roof. Eddie owned an aluminum Peterborough, 9.8 Merc. on the back, just like every other fishing boat in the region. Though locals thought of beavers as pests, you didn't call attention to yourself when trapping them.

By foot, they laid traps along the outlet stream then launched the boat into the marshy cove, setting more traps near the beaver house. They had their rods over the side. Sometimes summer people asked: catch any? But they meant fish, not large flat-tailed rodents.

They'd been trolling for about ten minutes when the kayak approached. As it moved closer, Eddie recognized the paddler, a psychologist who worked out of Kingston. Used to be, Eddie didn't hold much truck with that stuff. He'd still feel that way if it hadn't been for Meghan's problems last year, her nightmares and weight loss after a schoolmate died of cancer. It was Mary who suggested that their eldest daughter—a sweet, slim kid who read a lot—needed to talk to a professional. It had been hard for Eddie; he'd been raised to "keep things in the family" and reaching outside that intimate circle had caused him a few sleepless nights. But he recognized his limits; all the love in the world wasn't reassuring Meghan. The dark circles under her eyes appeared to be getting darker, or maybe it was just the new pallor of her skin. The night after Mary called and made the first therapy appointment, Eddie carried Meghan to bed from the couch where she'd fallen asleep after dinner. Was it his imagination or was she noticeably lighter? He felt the bones of her ribs against his arms. This was the physical confirmation that they needed help. The guy in the kayak, Dan, was the therapist who had worked with Meg.

"Catching any?" he asked as he came abreast, smiling in recognition at Eddie, but because of Brian's presence, behaving as if they'd never met.

"Not yet," said Eddie. "You live on this lake?"

"Yes. I do a circuit in the morning. Sometimes after dinner, too." The evening before, he added, a sizeable piece of bog had drifted the length of the lake, "Like a barge, like The Queen Mary, right down the middle of the lake."

Brian shrugged. "I seen it other places."

I've seen it Eddie corrected him silently. Brian tended to play the local yokel for effect.

"The root layer gets compromised when the water rises," Eddie said to Dan. "Due to beaver dams."

"Damned beavers, is more like it," added Brian, which made Dan laugh.

"We just laid a couple of traps," Eddie said. Later his brother gave him shit, but all Eddie would say was, "The guy's all right."

Meghan had gone to weekly sessions with Dan. She refused to relate what happened in therapy. "Her eyes are always red when I pick her up," Mary told Eddie. Over time these tears seemed less fatiguing and more of a release. Meghan stopped having nightmares and put a little flesh on her frame.

"She doesn't need me anymore," Dan told Mary at the end of the school year. Eddie respected that. It wasn't just healthy business; it was the business of health. Self-sufficiency. DIY.

It was what he'd come to realize about Jill Matthews, that she was just a woman trying to make it on her own. But during that first conversation, oh, they'd locked horns. He'd driven to her house and knocked on her front door. No answer. He was about to get back in the truck when she came around the corner of her house.

Pretty eyes and a generous mouth framed by lines. She had a trowel in her hand, a swipe of dirt on her cheek.

"I was just putting in bulbs," she explained.

"For the deer and the squirrels?"

"Oh I hope not," she'd said, with a comical grimace.

So he'd talked about chicken wire covering for the flowerbeds and suggested cayenne in the soil to deter the squirrels, all the stuff that Mary did. Jill Matthews was nodding, agreeing with him, appreciative. So he let the conversation segue to springtime and the pond and how her driveway might flood along with the corner of her garden, and he raised the subject of the beavers and "deterrents."

"You want to *kill* them?" she asked, her smile evaporating.

He responded obliquely: the former owner had trapped beavers every year.

She flung out her arms and the trowel kept going in an almost slow-motion arc out of her hand. He watched it land blade down, impaled in the grass, but she didn't seem to notice. "Tell me," she said, "why is killing such a part of the male mystique?"

He hated language like that: sarcastic, sophisticated. Call a fucking spade a spade, he thought. He raised and opened one hand in a gesture that meant 'stop' and turned on his heel.

"But she follows me," he told Mary later, "yapping away: 'We share this planet with other species.' I'm getting into my truck and she's going on about 'their territory.' So I said, 'Fine, see how you feel about sharing your laneway with the fish come spring.'" He shook his head and blew air out through his lips. "She says, 'Do you always have to have the last word?'"

"Ouch," said Mary, a look of sympathy on her face.

"And I lost it, Mare. I just said, 'Look here, I'm trying to save you from *sinking* this bloody property. You summer people are all the same. I *live* here. My family's been in this region for generations. I know what I'm talking about!'"

"Then she says, 'That doesn't give you dominion over the animals. You can't play God, deciding which ones live or die'. At that point, all I could do was drive away."

To his brothers he told a more colourful version: "She's just like the rest of 'em at the university." He held his beer bottle up so he could make quotes in the air: "Women's studies."

"Boot camp for bitches."

"Fucking one-breasted Amazons."

"No, she had both."

"Kind of a waste on a dyke," said Brian.

"Lezbo," said Dwight.

They were both looking at him, waiting. Dwight leaned forward and held his beer bottle like a microphone in front of his brother's lips.

Had he run out of epithets? Eddie drained his beer and grinned. "Carpet muncher."

She hired him the following spring.

"I thought about getting somebody else. But," she sighed, "better the devil you know ..."

He set the traps and noticed that she was conveniently absent when he came to empty them. But when he complained again to Mary, she shook her head.

"This isn't like you, Eddie. She called you; she ate crow. She paid you more than the job was worth. Let it go."

He thought he had. So why now, as he drives to her place, is he nervous?

She puts him at ease right away; none of the outside/inside rule for the "hired help."

"Thanks for coming, Eddie. I'd like you to look after the place while I'm away. I'm in California for part of the academic year. I'll be leaving in early December"

"That's nice," Eddie says, with a certain coolness.

"Oh I know, palm trees, sun, the ocean. Actually, I'm disappointed. I can't say no to the opportunity, but I was looking forward to staying right here."

He walks over to the old woodstove in the corner. "You'd have been cold."

"I need to buy a new one, I know."

"And that's just the beginning, I'm afraid."

"What else, Eddie?"

He outlines some options for insulation. "At minimum you need to insulate the attic, replace the windows, and weatherproof the doors." He catches himself, "I'm not trying to drum up business."

"Why not?"

It's a reasonable question. Because he's remembering their first encounters? Because he hates the hard sell. But mostly because he feels a sudden and inexplicable urge to protect her. From what?

She breaks through his silence. "Eddie, I need the place winterized for next year. This way, I'm out of your hair and I get to come home to a done deal in spring."

He tells Mary about it that night as they sit together in the living room after the kids are in bed. She's put on some music; they don't bother much with TV unless there's a game, and then Mary tends to face away from the screen and knit or read a book, but it's an established part of their relationship that they'll end up here for a couple of hours before retiring for the night.

Eddie takes his shirt off, offers his back to his wife for a rub. She obliges, kneading his spine up and down, warm fingers spreading over his shoulder blades. He lets out a low rumble of pleasure.

"I'm glad you're going to do the work for her," Mary says.

"Why?"

"I admire her for living out here, on her own. It's not easy for a woman."

"She's feisty enough," Eddie counters.

"So'm I, but out here, you know, Eddie, it's just more isolating for women, and I wouldn't want to do it without you."

"You're never gonna be without me, babe."

"But if something happened to one of us …"

They hear Sammy whimper, and both of them shift, Mary rising first. "I'll go. He didn't nurse very long the last time."

Eddie shivers, less from the temperature of the room—he built a nice fire in the fireplace earlier—than from Mary's conjuring a potential future he doesn't want to contemplate. They are a team, he and his wife, and he loves her and the kids and this house and their life rooted in this landscape that he has always known. Their energies, interests, and responsibilities cast themselves—like a net, like a spider web of connected strands, and sometimes there are moments that perfectly capture his contentment. Tonight before they sat out here, Eddie and Mary both read the girls bedtime stories, oh sure the girls are a little old for it, but they still love the ritual, one on each bed, two plots delivered *sotto voce*, braided together in the air below the white ceiling.

He knows he's lucky; there are marriages all around them in tepid limbo or worse. Dwight's wife suffers from depression. Brian recently confided that he and Carol haven't made love in a year. For Eddie to imagine his life here without Mary is, well, unthinkable. It's easier to feel a sense of satisfaction for what they do right: time together at the end of the day, regular sex, family outings. And Eddie has always helped out domestically, can't understand guys who think that doing the dishes is beneath them.

If he thinks about other people, single people—widowed, divorced, those who've never found a mate—it's with a sort of vague pity: they don't have what he and Mary have created. As for those who choose to be single, he just doesn't get it. Are they just too selfish to share, too stuck in their own ruts? But maybe it isn't a choice; maybe some people end up alone because they've lost something just like this. Enough, thinks Eddie, giving his head a shake and reaching for the tv remote.

A day later, he drops by Jill Matthew's house with a stove catalogue. There's no answer at the door, but her car is in the drive so he walks around the house. He sees her seated cross-legged on a stump, facing away from him and toward a stand of birch beside the pond. Her hand comes up, wipes at both cheeks. Eddie retreats quietly and deposits the catalogue in her mailbox. On the drive home it strikes him that watching her cry felt familiar, *deja vu*, but he's glad he walked away; he doesn't take her for one of those leaky types who cries socially. Then he forgets all about it in the distractions at home.

Before her departure, they arrange a number of visits so they can iron out details of the work he'll undertake. In the first months after she leaves, Eddie juggles the reno with other season-end jobs—closing cottages, helping his brothers to haul in floating docks, repairing roofs and putting up storm windows. He sends Jill Matthews brief but genial emails. She calls him every Friday. The talk is about materials and costs. She's cutting him lots of slack, trusting his decisions.

He is becoming intimate with her house, playing the radio and switching to CDs when the morning talk shows don't interest him. At noon he tends to turn off the call-in shows and read the paper after setting himself a place at the kitchen table and reheating the soup or leftovers that Mary packed that morning. These days it's invariably something *vegetarian*. Lately she's been on a real health kick, grains and beans and far too many greens for his liking, what Jenny calls spin-*ick* and aspara*guck*. If he has to drive to the hardware store or the building supply, he grabs a burger and leaves his quinoa pilaf in Jill's fridge.

One day as he's getting ready to go home, he pulls out his wallet, tucks two crisp $100 bills in a kitchen drawer. Guilt money—it's the amount he overcharged her for the driveway draining last spring. He thinks about adding a note, "from the Beaver God." But no, let her think she put it there and forgot, or that it's left over from renovation expenditures.

He moves stuff around: bookshelves into the middle of the room, furniture away from the walls and piled under drop sheets. She's cleared the side tables of knick-knacks and packed away what she could. What's left isn't a lot of work; her decor is Spartan, second-hand furniture, rag rugs, a few old ceramic jugs.

She's taken the artwork off the walls. He finds a stack of framed paintings leaning against a box in the hall closet. It doesn't seem like snooping to look, since they've all been on the walls before. A few modern prints and a small wooded scene. He runs his hands over the box. He wants to open it, but he shuts the closet and returns to the task at hand, replacing the windows in the smaller of the bedrooms.

There are nail holes in the wall above the bed and the small pine dresser, and it suddenly occurs to him that there are way more than can be accounted for by the frames he found. He wonders if they, whatever *they* are, are in the box.

"No," he says, aloud, walking into the hall and on into the kitchen where he steps out of his work overalls and slings them over a chair. The next day he walks in the door and straight into the larger bedroom. He tries to pretend he's only checking if the walls are board and batten, or drywall—the house is a mix—but he's really looking for nail holes. There are dozens of them in one wall alone. He feels again that urge to see the photos or artworks that are important and yet private enough to be removed. Are they of a man Jill Matthews used to know or was married to once? It's more than curiosity; he's actually beginning to feel jealous.

He makes himself think of Mary. She has a healthy appetite for sex, and it is she, more than he, who introduces variations. Sometimes she puts on a lace teddy or brings a bottle of wine to bed. He's a lucky man. Jill Matthews is an attractive woman; he'll give her that. But his feelings are getting out of hand; this is not a line of thought or fantasy that he wants to pursue.

A day or two on and he needs access to that closet for some reason. He slides the box out and opens it before he can censor the move, laying its contents—ten framed photos—on a paint-splattered drop sheet. By the time he has the last out, a lump has formed in his throat.

The photographs are of a boy. In the first of them, a younger and longer-haired Jill is holding her infant son and smiling. Radiantly. As the photos continue and the boy becomes a toddler, his resemblance to his mother starts to show. Both of the last photos to come out of the box show the same child looking thin and drawn. In one, a birthday cake holds eight candles, but the backward baseball cap can't cover his baldness. Cancer. It's impossible to know if a father has been edited out of this selection or if he was never there in the first place.

All thoughts of windows and work are abandoned for the moment. There are no more boxes in the hall or bedroom closet, though he pushes aside shoes and summer dresses. He's walking toward her dresser when he catches sight of himself in its mirror, the flush of colour up his neck and cheeks. A carpenter might need to open a closet or move a dresser, but it's quite another thing to rummage through a woman's lingerie drawer. *Edward Pilcher, you are beyond the pale.* It isn't his wife's voice but his mother's. He backs out of the room and doesn't stop moving till he's outside on the drive.

He bends over with his hands on his knees and takes a deep breath.

Whatever's happening, he thinks, it has to stop. He goes back inside, repacks the box, and puts it away. Then he starts on the living room windows, turning the radio up, and singing along to hits from the 70s. When Dwight shows up to help remove the old wood stove, they get to it quickly, heaving it into Eddie's truck before rewarding themselves with a couple of cold beers.

That night Mary turns to him. He pulls her in and feels the familiar comfort of her warm body against his own, her bare breasts as she wriggles out of her nightgown, his answering erection. But as he snuggles down to take her nipple into his mouth, he thinks of the balding boy. His penis goes limp.

It's happened the odd time before, either because he was getting sick or had drunk too much beer. Mary would tease him about his "tired monkey," and they'd cuddle until they went to sleep. He waits now for that easy forgiveness as they face each other, lying together in the dark. But she rolls over without a word. It's uncharacteristic of her, not that she turned toward him earlier, but that she has turned away now, not even a peck goodnight on the cheek. He looks at his wife's shoulders, a wall he can't breach because he can't begin to explain tonight's preoccupation. Somewhere, in the back of his mind, he recognizes a warning ping, like a penny down a dry well.

I am surrounded by sadness, he thinks, and the thought surprises him. He turns his back to Mary's and falls into a troubled sleep.

The other photos find him. He's moving the bed away from the wall in the spare room so he can get at the baseboards. One of the legs of the bed pushes against something. He gets down on his hands and knees. Beneath the box spring is a small, old-fashioned cardboard suitcase. He slides it out. His mind is clear; he'll put it somewhere, either in the linen cupboard or in the bedroom closet, but as he picks it up, grabbing the small leather handle, the suitcase opens and what's in it spills onto the hardwood floor: a pile of boy's clothing, a hospital bracelet, a package of photos.

The pictures he looks at now are harder to bear than the others: the larger Jill's smile, the more obvious the ravages of disease on the small face beside hers. The boy's eyes are deep pools above bruised shadows. In one, Joseph—that's the name on the bracelet, but to Eddie he is already Joey—is wearing a Santa hat and reading *The Grinch Who Stole Christmas*. His mother is lying beside him. Beyond her shoulder, there's an out-of-focus apparatus, probably an iv. How many nights did she sleep on a cot beside that bed, one hand through the rails so that the tip of her finger touched her son?

Who took the pictures? Eddie wonders.

He has some things to pick up at the hardware store. It's a clear day. They've already had one snowfall, but this morning has opened onto a brilliant blue sky, and the air feels warm enough to sit outside. Eddie makes his purchases. Afterward, with his arm out the window at a red light, he inhales the smoky tang of burgers. There's a container of tofu stroganoff in the fridge at Jill's. No contest! Eddie turns into the Burger King lot. In less than ten minutes he's outside again with a cheeseburger and fries, heading toward the picnic tables. Two of the tables are occupied, one by a young mother with her preschooler. At the other a couple are leaning toward each other over their cardboard trays. In spite of the warm sun, the woman, whose back is to Eddie, has her sweatshirt hood pulled up.

It's the kayaking therapist from Inverary. Since Eddie set those traps he's run into Dan a couple of times, once on the lake and the second time with his wife at the Price Chopper. What's her name? It starts with a K. Kirsten? Kaitlin? Eddie's about to say hello but hesitates. Whatever the couple is talking about, it looks serious. A marital argument perhaps, or this is its fast-food reconciliation. And just as it occurs to him that maybe it isn't the wife, a breeze rolls a crumpled napkin the length of their table and the woman who is not Kaitlin turns to grab it. Eddie catches a glimpse of profile behind the pale blue hood.

It's Mary. She and Dan are engrossed in their conversation and don't notice Eddie or his immediate about-face, his heart-pounding march to his truck. He tosses his burger bag on the seat and shoves the large pop into the drink holder so hard the Coke spurts out of the straw and all over his hand. "Damn!" His hand is dripping as he turns the key in the ignition and yanks the gearshift. The truck tires actually *squeal* as he reverses out of the parking lot.

He licks the Coke off his hand. His heart is banging in his chest.

Slow down, he says to himself, maybe they're talking about Meghan. But Mary has been acting strange lately, distant and preoccupied, and what if she's, if they're …

Suddenly, more than anything he wants to hear Jill Matthew's voice.

He's been calling LA between the weekly check-ins, more than he needs to, perhaps. Their talk is no longer just about costs and materials. Jill speaks of her pleasure in being by the ocean and marvels at the preponderance of snack foods in American supermarkets. He told her when the maples and sumac turned colour, and reports bird sightings at her feeder in the yard; she left a fifty-pound bag of seed and strict instructions to keep it filled. The day of that first snow fall, she asked him to describe the texture of the snow, and he obliged: "clumpy" and "tingling on the skin."

"And on your tongue?"

He laughs. "Oh yeah."

"I do that, too," she said.

He was silent for a minute, conjuring a vision of her outside her new double-glazed windows, head thrown back. Did she, too, sense the tiny erotic tug down the phone lines?

Even when he isn't talking to her, he feels something about the place. It echoes her presence. And her son's, though the boy was never there. The house, Eddie realizes, is filled with longing.

He finishes off the burger before he gets out of the truck. As for the image of Mary and Dan leaning together across a picnic table, *he can't think about that now*. But he does anyway, and the more he tries to find an explanation for it, the more he sees it morph into another man, himself, and another woman, Jill, and they are reaching for each other's hands, leaning in ... To dispel both the imagined scene and what he actually saw, or at least to expend the manic energy building inside his chest, Eddie spends the next two hours ripping out a wall. When he reaches for the phone to dial Jill's California number, he tells himself it's because they need to discuss the slate shelf beneath the wood stove, and while the phone is ringing he allows himself the following physiological observations: his heart is racing and his breathing is louder, perhaps, than normal, but that could be the effort he's expended on the old plaster. She's not there. Disappointed, he locks up for the day and drives home with a CD of Brian Adams playing full-blast. The minute he's out of his truck and walking towards his house he's the wronged husband. Mary's with another man, with the therapist that treated their daughter? Today!? He kicks off his boots and hangs his windbreaker over a hook in the mudroom. He enters the steamy room, potatoes boiling over unnoticed while Sammy pulls himself up by means of a dishtowel over the stove door.

"Jesus, Mary!" Eddie shouts, striding across the kitchen.

He snatches up his son, who begins to cry. Patting Sammy on the back and holding him close, Eddie turns, sees the roasting pan beside the sink, the chicken sitting in it, pale and uncooked. He turns the potatoes down. "Where are the girls?"

She's staring into space, oblivious to his noisy entrance and question, oblivious even to the danger her baby was in. He feels something then, or rather the lack of something, as if the robust and vibrant core of their house—air usually buoyant, crisscrossed with cooking smells, children's voices, and

Mary's efficient energy—has collapsed. Eddie Pilcher stands in the empty-aired kitchen and stares at his wife's slack expression, and senses that life as he knew it, as he had been able to take it for granted, is over. Something else is about to begin. He doesn't know what it is.

Needed to put her emotions on hold; needed to not think about it. Needed to be sure. Needed to wean—and here she swallowed hard, the first real show of emotion that evening—Sammy before the treatments started.

"Why didn't you tell me, Mary? We're partners. You're my …" Hands up, swinging at the air." This affects … everything."

The kids were in bed. He was standing, looking across the coffee table and down at her where she sat, un-Mary-like in her stiffness, at the edge of the couch. They had both been talking softly except for that last outburst.

"I didn't have the words," she paused and raised her hands as if to hold her chest, but she stopped, placed them firmly back in her lap, folded together. When she spoke again her voice was tired. "Words … for it. Cancer."

There. The word hung in the air in the middle of the room, their living room, their *life*! And his mind was reeling. *TMI*, it's what people said now, *too much information*, but this really was too much at once, starting with what sent her to the doctor in the first place.

"Lots of women have lumps, Eddie, I wasn't concerned at first." Then the subsequent tests: a mammography, then an ultrasound, then the needle biopsy, and another when the first proved inconclusive, and finally, the confirmed diagnosis yesterday.

Yesterday? It took a second for that to sink in. He stopped his pacing for a moment and gave a little twitch, like a deer in the bush when it has been spotted. Last night, she'd put Sammy in his arms and said, "I just have to make a call." She'd called Dan.

"Dan?" he said now, surprise and hurt in his voice. "You told him first?"

"Eddie," she raised her eyebrows—not the customary wiggle, but an expression both stern and disdainful that made him suddenly aware that he had been on the verge of, no, he actually *had been* scolding her. Get a grip, he warned himself, your wife just told you she has cancer. He took a step around the coffee table, knelt, and drew her to him. It took a moment before the stiffness in her torso became a slow bend.

"Telling *you* makes it a reality, Eddie." She was crying now, softly. "Don't you see? And now we have to find a way to tell the kids."

And later in the darkness of their bedroom, as he held her and kissed the top of her head, she said, "And during this whole time you've been odd, Eddie, sort of distant. Maybe I've been angry with you because, oh, I dunno, because you weren't reading my mind. It gave me a focus, something else to think about."

"Mary, I'm sorry."

"So am I." A few minutes passed, and he thought she might have fallen asleep. He was beginning to drop off when she made a quick movement, taking his chin in her hand and turning his face toward hers in the shadowy light. "Don't pity me, Eddie. I couldn't bear the thought of it being 'the glue' between us."

He said nothing for a moment. How could he have considered anyone else, how could he have betrayed his life. "I love you, Mary."

Eddie Pilcher is talking on the phone. Out his kitchen window, a cherry tree is in bloom. Fat rosettes of pink-white blossoms, colour so pretty and preening it can't possibly last. Across the table from him, Meghan is cutting toast for her younger brother.

He catches her attention, holds up a finger and mouths, "One hour?" She nods. They have developed a shorthand in recent weeks. It saddens him at times, that she is maturing so fast, and it makes him proud too, to see her capabilities, the changes wrought in his once fragile daughter. Maybe those nightmares were a rehearsal for her mother's illness, this new presence in the house. It's amazing what you can get used to, he thinks. On "hospital" days, when Mary gets chemo, or when she can't stray too far from bed and a bucket, Meghan helps her father in the kitchen and reads to Jenny while Eddie puts Sammy to bed.

Into the receiver, Eddie says, "I'll drop by now with the key."

Jill meets him in the driveway, steps forward as he climbs out of the cab of his truck and envelops him in a hug. "It's so beautiful, Eddie, all of it. Thank you."

He's spent so many months staring at her photos, staring at the Jill of several years back, that he's forgotten the lines on her forehead, the smile creases around her eyes and mouth, the amount of silver in her hair. Her skin is tanned from her time in California. There's something else; it isn't until they're drinking tea in the living room that he gets it: he's looking at a healthy woman. He fumbles the cup onto the table and covers his face with his hands.

"Eddie, what is it?"

Once he starts, he can't stop: the tests and surgery, Mary's stoic silence leading up to the diagnosis.

"We used to tell each other the important stuff," he says, adding silently: *and if she hadn't gotten sick, I might have told her about you.*

"Cancer brings out different things in people."

He tells her, now, about finding the photos of her son, and the fear he feels every night when he cradles Mary in his arms. He doesn't bother to brush away the tears that are coursing down his cheeks.

Partway through his outpouring, she moves across to sit beside him on the couch. Her arm comes around his shoulders. "I know," she says. "I know." Does she mean everything he's experienced in the past ten months, or just that she understands his need to cry?

And when he's calmer, cried out, and they've walked around the house and talked over all the changes, they arrive in the kitchen. She mentions the money in the drawer.

"Is it yours, Eddie?"

"Nope."

She looks stumped, says she can't recall leaving any cash around.

As he drives away from her house he looks out over the cove. No matter how many you trap, no matter how many dams you break apart, the beavers come back. The surface of the water is broken, now, by a flat head. He angles the truck onto the gravel shoulder and turns off the engine, watching the widening V. For a moment he is the long-ago dreamy boy, staring over the lake. Something startles the beaver; it slaps and dives. When the last of the ripples clear, Eddie turns the key in the ignition, pulls back onto the highway and drives home. He parks in front of the garage, releases his seatbelt and checks in the rearview mirror to see if his eyes are red. Then he gets out of his truck and walks across the lawn.

ACKNOWLEDGEMENTS

River and lake travel is a narrative. These stories would not exist without Frank de Jong, my paddling partner for sixteen and a half years. In between trips he answered innumerable questions pertaining to the natural world. Karen and Ian Whyte provided companionship, guidance, and inspiration on camping trips, and were generous with wildflower lists, photographs, and excerpts from their travel journals. The oldest story in the collection owes its genesis and its heart to Iain Hillier. Patti Morden told me of her friend's death by hypothermia and that story never let me go; later, Barb Scott provided details about life in a seismic camp. Veronica Koopmans, MD clarified the symptoms of hypothermia. Kalevi Hannila helped with research on meromixis. My neighbour Don Armstrong talked to me about moose hunting, brought over his tackle box and spoke at length with Ruth Henderson and me about sixth sense. Those talks were the genesis for "White Crow." Spaces to write were generously provided by Marney Malabar, Grant Carmichael, Moya Foley (La Fortuna, Ecuador), Cathy Vakil, and Terry Mauer (Inverary Lake), and Daryl Aitken (Jack Lake). This manuscript was worked on at the Banff Centre for the Arts under the mentorship of Edna Alford, and during a three-month residency at Berton House, Dawson City (with support from Yukon Arts Council). Thoughtful feedback on one or more stories was provided by Alice Zorn, Alison Watt, Alayna Munce, Irene Guilford, Dorothy Speak, Dorothy Goulah, Isabelle Gutmanis, Jean McKay, and Grant Carmichael. Thanks to Scott Peterson for seeing parallels at the eleventh hour.

This book had two editors. Sue Macleod asked important questions, caught grammatical lapses, and engaged me in deep discussion over each story. She helped me believe in their eventual publication. Helen Humphreys offered crucial insights and solutions and helped me hone the collection. I am indebted to them both.

I am lucky in my friendship with Maureen Harris. Our conversations, literary and otherwise, keep me on the writer's path. Anna Payne made the cover possible. I am grateful for her patience, her eye, and her considerable skills.

The story "Downhill" was published under the title "Real Weather" in *EVENT*, Volume 38 #1, Spring/Summer 2009.

My sincere thanks to the Tightrope team, especially Jim Nason and Heather Wood.

Tallulah and Grady Shin drift with me around a green cove in a green canoe. They are all light.

ABOUT THE AUTHOR

PHOTO: Zenia Buzanko

Kelley Aitken is a writer, artist and teacher. Her book *Love in a Warm Climate* (The Porcupine's Quill, 1998) was nominated for the Commonwealth Prize, Best First Book. Kelley has lived in the Philippines, Ecuador and various parts of Canada. Born in British Columbia, Kelley makes her home in Toronto where she teaches drawing at the Art Gallery of Ontario.